What Your Mom Didn't Tell You
Life, Men, Love, Dating, Sex and Relationships

By Chiedza Mavangira

What Your Mom Didn't Tell You: *Life, Men, Love, Dating, Sex and Relationships*
First published in the United States of America by BlackMoney Brands LLC™

Copyright © BlackMoney Brands LLC, 2019

For permissions contact:
www.blackmoneybrands.com
blackmoneybrands@gmail.com

ISBN: 9781699710333

Edited by
Itayi Garande
itayig@hotmail.com

Dear dreamer out there

Never give up on your dreams.

Please find below the testimonials of people who have touched my life. From my favorite English teacher, to my mentor for the award winning documentary on Discovery, to the headmistress of my high school, to the first application I made to a writing college in the USA that turned me down..

Now my moment by God's grace has arrived.

Grab your Amazon copy with a boom!!!

Head bowed

CTM

Who is Chiedza Tawuchira Mavangira (CTM)?

CTM is a model, actress, luxury realtor, businesswoman and author. She currently lives in Laguna Beach, California. She lives with her fiancé and college attending twenty-one year old son.

Acknowledgements

I had no idea that the man sitting in a wheelchair across from me would change my life.

It's a bright afternoon in the City of Angels and I'm working on my third documentary entitled "The Felony of Art". I have one gorgeous camera babe who is also my sound tech and lighting person. It's a sexy two woman band in six inch heels! Shortly, I shall meet a woman who survived a plane crash and stepped out of a raging fire to find her life purpose, a handsome young computer genius who crashed his fast red Ferrari and found his calling as a gifted painter and, I guess, a young woman from a city called Bulawayo in a far away country called Zimbabwe who followed her heart and found her voice as a writer.

To find out what happened next, stay tuned in for our documentary, "The Felony of Art".

To find out what happened a couple of years later when, out of the blue and serendipitously, I reconnected with one of the above-mentioned folks flip to the cover of this book.

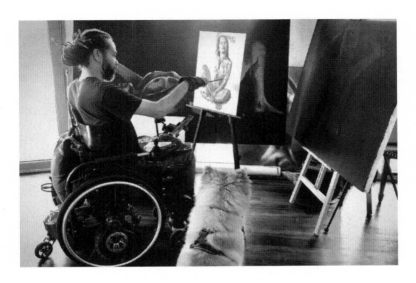

Artist Richard "Dicky" Bell

Meet Richard "Dicky" Bell, the artist to whom I am deeply humbled to give credit for the book cover to my first book. Head bowed. "Hey. It would be nice to work on something together sometime," Dicky suggested in his calm unassuming gentle way.

"Sure!" I responded without hesitation or much thought. Little did I know that those simple words would manifest themselves on canvas as a masterpiece. With the undeniable skill of the old masters, Dicky Bell places his paintbrushes in his hand gloves and paints without consideration to what others would see as the obstacle of his limited mobility.

"Sometimes I get my paint brushes from Home Depot," he said to me with amusement, lighting up his voice and throwing me a dashing smile.

Apparently, the magic is not in the instruments used, but I'm the blessed hands that hold them.

"... and that's the day that I learned how to correct an error on canvas. I had no idea that my Uncle Raymond Howell was teaching me skills that I would develop later as I found my own techniques as an artist," Dicky Bell said to me.

It goes without saying that the rest is history. I had reached a writer's block when I met Dicky Bell and I felt like I would never materialize my dream of being a writer. Even with the witty input of my writing partner and sister, Nattu Emma Mavangira, I was stuck.

Then God sent me and angel and that's the moment that my dreams came true. Through working with Dicky Bell and watching his tenacity, passion, compassion, devotion and surrender to his gift and higher calling, I found the courage to do the same.

"I don't blame God for what happened to me. I celebrate the gift I discovered. I love to paint!" Dicky said with a serene smile.

I no longer had an excuse to be a victim to growing up in the third world country or any of my life tragedies but only the inspiration to be great. It is with great joy and humility that I ask you as my beloved reader to enjoy my first book.

Chiedza and Emma Mavangira with Brandi *(in the middle)*

It is with deep appreciation that I would like to thank my sister and co-author Emma Nattu Mavangira for all the times she read my work sitting on a bus, train or cab going to work and told me it was "so juicy!"

No one else in the world would have given me their home, heart and couch for many a night to sit on the floor with Kimora, my puppy, and scribble away for days at a time, except my best friend Brandi Bratcher.

Left to Right: Sister Emma Nattu, mom Stella and CTM

To my mom, Stella Mavangira, remember that time when I wrote an essay in grade school that my teacher and classmates accused me from stealing in a book and my you said "Awesome! Now you know you are gifted!"?

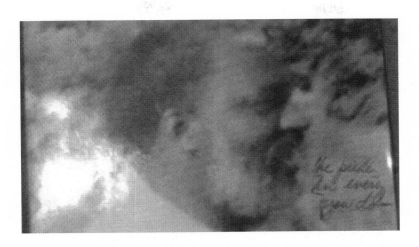

Dad Zebron Tawuchira Mavangira

To my Dad Zebron Tawuchira Mavangira, I attribute my faith that anything is possible. He had the courage to leave his small village of Buhera and set out to make his dreams come true!

Johnny Buss and Doctor Buss of the LA Lakers with CTM (middle)

To Johnny Buss and Doctor Buss of the LA Lakers who was an avid reader and always asked me: "So what have you being writing lately young lady?!"

Dr. Pat Allen

To Doctor Pat Allen for her stern look and gracious spirit: "What can I do for you young lady that God has not already done?!"

To my brothers, Let-It-Be Mavangira and Atheling Reginald Peace-Be Mavangira who taught me grace under fire and to always be myself.

To my favorite Math teacher Mrs Gurajena who taught me how to strut across any room like a runway model.

And to all my many loves, teachers, friends and mentors who have always believed in me.

To the only English teacher who ever believed in me so much so that she took extra time away from school to help me polish up my writing skills, wherever in the world you are Mrs King, I love you so much and I pray that you will read this book. It exists because of your passion as an English teacher.

At Rivet Entertainment where I was part of the team that won an award-winning documentary on Discovery, I humbly thank all the energetic and brilliant people I had the pleasure and honor to work with, especially Paul Laussier and Bill Latka.

I thank the amazing RedCarpetTips creator, celebrity stylist Charlie Lapson for giving me my first shot on the red carpet.

To the iconic Jose Eber and Karl Seelig of Rodeo Drive, thank you so much for showing the ins and out of the most glamorous things on earth.

To my son, Ivano Mavangira, you are my love note from Heaven and the reason that I still believe in God.

To Nyasharai R, thank you for believing in me and being there for me in my darkest hours.

To my editor Itayi Garande, I am eternally grateful! You are the big brother I thought I had lost, but was given a second chance with again.

To Richard McCay, "I'm abouta do this boo!" Lol. Thank you so much for everything! I'd like to thank all my beloved connections on social media who help to shape me every day and make me a better person.

And last and most importantly, to my God up in Heaven and my ancestors in the wind, I thank you that I finally found my way home.

Foreword

Chiedza

You are a romantic junkie who binges on old editions of *Cosmopolitan*. You are addicted to dog-eared tattered paperbacks, with underlined juicy paragraphs, and brawny half-naked men who catch delirious women with bewitching love spells.

You get tipsy with your girlfriends, stalk your ex fiancé's new girlfriend on social media, and drunk text men who seem undesirable in the sober light of day.

Your inner-circle is an illegal blonde financial advisor, a sassy tomboy accountant, and a stuck up real estate agent who shows houses in red tailored pants. Not to mention, your drop-dead gorgeous sister.

You've watched more "Sex in the City" reruns than you care to admit and you don't see anything wrong with meeting your future husband at a local funeral parlor.

You think at any given moment "the one" might just walk into your pretty picture, and you still believe in love at first sight.

Sound familiar? If this is relatable, then you may have a bunch of things your mamma forgot to tell you...

Hunny, this book is definitely for you.

On the other hand, if you are just plain boring, with no friends or social life, and desperate to find a spark, this book is also for you.

My tribe and I have read trillions of "How to" articles on dating, love, relationships, and men. We spend our Wednesday nights at Dr. Pat Allen love seminars and we can't help but wonder if we are an astrological match with so-and-so. What can I say? We are self-confessed hopeless romantics. Even common sense is not a cure. But we are about to put our big girl pants on and welcome a candid talking to from our Vatete.

As a very passionate relationship blogger, I have the unique privilege to travel half-way across the world; from the baptizing grassroots of my home village, to the glossy tiles of Rodeo Drive. And in these ventures I've learned, love is love is love.

Unlike most of you, my sister and I had the privilege of spending many magical moments with a gaggle of aunts who taught us ancient wisdom on love.

What makes this book the love bible for women on dating, relationships and sex, is that it is the combined experiences of real women just like you, who have been chewed up and spit back out into the dating world to try again. *What Your Mamma Didn't Tell Ya* is the first volume in a set of 10 volumes within the Naked Truth Series.

When it comes to love, there are no rules, but there are laws of engagement. These are as fundamental as gravity, which one cannot ignore. Before you fall in love, consider the real possibility of hitting the ground hard.

The unique point of view of this guide is not based on clinical and lofty studies that live in the safe haven of academia. Instead, consider my tribe to be the guinea pig, and our real lives to be your private love laboratory. We have tested every theory and made every mistake. With that said, you are now privileged to the grand wisdom and voice of my love tribe my dearest sage, Vatete.

Unlike in my traditional African culture, a lot of women do not have the experience of being schooled by their Vatete. Vatete is the sound voice of reason. Vatete holds all the secrets to love, sex, dating and men. Vatete is our lost rite of passage from childhood to womanhood. We do not have the luxury of our village Vatete anymore, but we have access to the love bible which she could have written herself. This love bible borrows from the ancient wisdom of women, to shed light on some of the most perplexing love questions of all times.

"How do I know if he loves me?"
"How do I know if he is "the one"?
"How do I heal my broken heart?"

And more.

This love bible will give you all the tools that you need to win at love.

Introduction
The Secret Love Potion

Artist's impression of Chiedza

In my Shona culture and the creed of my family, a woman of great substance is ready for marriage and a lifelong partnership with another only after she has accomplished her own dreams and goals.

My sister Nattu and I had achieved that much by the Grace of God. We had both traveled to a foreign country where we knew no-one and started a brand new life. At the pinnacle of this success, Nattu was working in Fashion and Beauty and I was working in Media and Entertainment. We also both had the privilege of sitting on the Board of Directors for our evolving family businesses. We were schooled in the ways of American culture by virtue of living in the States now, but it was time for us to reconnect with our true authentic roots.

"Vatete!" Nattu and I jumped off the bed and flew into loving arms.

"Girls! I missed you so much. I thought this place had swallowed you whole. You must start to visit the village more often."

"Yes Tete. Please forgive us we have being so busy with going to school, getting good jobs, starting our businesses…"

"And yet no rings. Mmmmh."

We giggled knowing that there was no accomplishment greater than this to Vatete and it was pointless for us to argue with her.

"But we are happy." I said back, with a little harsher tone than I intended.

"Speak for yourself Chi. I want a man and many babies Tete." Nattu pulled Vatete down into the haven of pillows, romance novels and magazines piled up on the bed.

"Well you are no longer children and this is why I am here. You are now the sacred age of *mhandara* and you are giving off signals to nature of which you must be prepared to respond."

"Signals?" We asked in union, eyeing each other from our near-identical eyes, but still secretly thinking the other one was prettier.

"Vatete it's all so complicated." Nattu said

"I wish that there was just a love potion!" I chimed in, taking a sip of my wine and ignoring my Vatete's disapproving look.

"But my dear there is a love potion…" Vatete answered with a mischievous grin.

"What?!" we asked springing forward and staring her squarely in the eyes.

"Girls, girls you must settle down and relax." She shrugged off her shawl settling neatly in-between us like the crown jewel of wisdom that had come to make our grooming as young women complete.

2

"Chi...why don't you begin by reading me one of these blogs I hear your write about on love... after which I will begin my very short lesson for the day."

Never Be Sold On Love: 10 Reasons Why

"He used to hang on my every word." She thought.

Who is the unscrupulous salesman who sold you on your belief systems, a counterfeit dream and a broken promise out of his beat up bag of a mouth?

In life someone is always trying to sell you something. We live in the world of sophisticated multiple-level marketing, brilliant social media advertising campaigns and the perpetual erosion of our attention to the ever enigmatic and larger than life penetrative TV and radio gurus.

Your dentist is trying to sell you a whiter smile, Louis Vuitton a bag you must kill to possess, and the lady next door has a bottle of Nerium anti-aging cream you have to try. Religion is selling you God. Politicians are selling you freedom and economists wealth.

From the book shelves, writers are selling their ideas. From the street corners, pimps are selling you flesh.

From the newsstands, the world is selling you fear. Today I will disenchant you. The best anti-medicine to sales is purchasing. There is a difference in mentality between being sold on something and deciding to purchase something. A sale is done to you. A purchase is done by you. One empowers the salesman and the other empowers you. Today I am challenging you to purchase a new mentality. Below is the eulogy to a dying breed: The Death of a Salesman.

#1 Here lies a salesman who was a talker. The gift of gab is synonymous to being a successful salesman. A salesman's voice will make or break his success when it comes to selling you love. Your ears come with a 100 percent guaranteed warranty to protect you if you use them. Listen to the tone of voice. Read in-between the lines. Make a mental note of inconsistencies.

Is the language too flowery, but with no roots? Is the energy aligned to the magnitude of the words? Is the eye contact too mirror-rehearsed or are these eels of eyes swimming away every-time a body with a pulse walks by? The great thing about the voice of a salesman is that it comes out of his body. If it could be projected from a machine and fine-tuned to perfection you'd be dead in the water.

But because it comes out of a living human body, the voice is subject to a trillion neurobiological influences which cannot be manipulated. The first thing a voice will reveal upon first burp is the mental and emotional state of the speaker. A slow steady voice will infer a premeditated and controlled delivery. This comes out of a stronger-willed, calculated and smarter mind. This is also most likely to be a quality of the most pretentious and charming of these breed of talkers. A hurried, clumsy speech will show an impulsive on-the-spot approach to selling you on love.

A tense voice is as a result of the vocal cords tightening up and usually indicative of latent anger issues. A high pitched annoying voice is off a lower level 'used-car type' salesman. The tone of voice reveals a lower level of testosterone which makes this man less attractive to women chemically. This is a high volume salesman meaning he has to talk to 100 women to get one fluke of a yes. This type will usually be in a big hurry to get you into bed before you change your mind. This is a big No! Men like this usually need to pay for sex so are more prone to having STIs. This is the partial profile of someone capable of really hurting you physically as well because years of rejection build up a latent hate for women. Voices are like sponges. They absorb the character of a man over time.

#2 Here lies a salesman who has confidence and a touch of arrogance. Everyone of this breed is confident. That's average. To be brilliant, he will need much more. He will need a touch of arrogance because this is what will push him over the edge of indecision into a resounding yes when he sells you on love.

Learn to study the character of a man because in it will lie the encyclopedia of everything you will ever need to know about him. Although confidence might be God-given, arrogance is always cultivated. It takes discipline to cultivate anything. It takes talent to pull off an ovation of performance.

The only reason women fall in love is because somewhere along the line they were sold on some 'false guarantees'. Was it the promise of forever, fun or security? Whatever it is, it will not be backed up by action. Anytime a delivery is impeccably perfect, examine its authenticity because only a lot of practice has made it this good. Ask yourself this: How can you trust someone who lies to themselves? After all, a true salesman projects an absolute lack of fear, yet this man is afraid of commitment and of true love. That's a deal-breaker boo.

#3 Here lies a salesman who had empathy. The ability to mimic your emotions is the sign of a great salesman. He will make you feel like you are connected and that he understands whatever you are feeling or going through. Brilliant war strategy because once your walls come down, it will be your emotional waterloo.

Throw a dog a fake bone. He is so intuitive; he should be able to tell the difference. Parade a range of emotions which are far from your heart and then sit back and make a very clinical observation. How does he respond? What does he say? What does he not do? Action is the only thing which bridges a Salesman from an Alpha. A True Alpha will call you as promised, Send that car on time and follow up on that evening out. A salesman will tell you he will call you, he will suggest that he might take you out somewhere nice and he will want you to imagine your upcoming vacation together.

The true test is when you express your disappointment suddenly. You will either anger or annoy him. Wait a minute what happened to "understanding how you feel"? Exactly.

#4 Here lies a salesman who had a great briefcase. What is a classical image of a salesman without his scuffed shoes and beat up briefcase? Lost in the passage of time. You know a witch by their familiar... the black cat which follows them around, the pointed hat on the counter top or the broom leaning near the door. Take your pick. A briefcase and scuffed shoes that a salesman makes. A man with holes is his soul cannot love you. A shoe with holes in it cannot walk the journey of a hundred miles.

If his heart has being battered by life, it's a beat-up briefcase which cannot hold anything good for you except perhaps some papers for you to sign on the dotted line. Signed, sealed and delivered to the devil.

*I understand that I will have my heart broken. Sign here, date, time

#5 Here lies a salesman who solved problems. Keep your problems to yourself as they will make you an easy target. When a salesman discovers what you need sold to you, you will be a goner. What does your heart desire? Children and a family? Love and security? Companionship and encouragement?

A great salesman knows that the way to sell you on love is to offer you the solutions to all your problems. This is precisely what they call selling your soul to the devil. Beware the man who offers you the whole world on a silver plate. There will be a tragic price to pay. The best way to get rid of a salesman is to not be in the market for anything.

#6 Here lies a salesman who knew how to inspire trust. You would not be in any danger of losing your heart if there was no trust involved, the first and only rule to love is Trust No One. Men are not infallible creatures, so you set yourself up for certain failure when you trust people. Like Dr. Pat Allen loves to say, 'None of us are worth loving or marrying.' Truly!

What you might want to do is to trust in someone's overall trustworthy record. This takes time to build. One thing even the best salesman cannot do is to manipulate the passage of time. In time, all things will be illuminated by the truth.

#7 Here lies a salesman who knew how to create urgency. The oldest sales technique in the world is to create a false sense of urgency. Now. Immediately. Right away. There are no limited offers on love as long as your life has not expired. A broken heart is the condition of a sense of false security. There will never be another person like your first love. The first kiss was earth shattering. How could love ever be this perfect? No man will ever hold you like this again. As romantic as it sounds it's a load of bull. In fact, the next one is always better than the last. It's the essence of lessons learned that makes love sweeter.

#8 Here lies a salesman who knew how to close the deal. Only closers break hearts. Never let anyone close you. Keep your options open; know your entire emergency exists and run if you must. Closing someone is a psychological act.

Once a great salesman makes you decide to love him, he has closed you. Your mind will guide your heart and your heart will lead your actions. Your actions will, beyond a shadow of doubt, seal the deal.

#9 Here lies a salesman who had passion. Passion is the jet fuel that skyrockets a great salesman. The thing with passion is that it is a beautiful thing. You can fall in love with a passionate frog and be repelled by a lazy prince.

A salesman will have enough passion to take you to the ends of the earth and back, and if you do not have your own passion, we will bury you here. Find what makes you tick. Passion is the breastplate of protection against which cupids arrows are extinguished. When you are driven and passionate, you need not be consumed by the motives of others. You cannot be sold on love. Passion is the strongest currency in life, and with it, you can buy the happy ending of your picking and not be sold on a bootleg version.

#10 Here lies a salesman who had a hunting mentality. The antithesis to being gullible is to understand why it makes you an easy target to being sold on love. A great salesman has a hunting mentality and what this entails is to be constantly in hot pursuit of his prey. He never sleeps or rests. He has no 'downtime' or 'off' button. He needs to conquer and he is focused in this endeavor.

The salesman is the evil alter-ego of an Alpha man. He sells to sell. He lives to make you a believer. He is more obsessed with the number of conquests than their quality. If you are prey, he will spot you from a million miles away. He will smell your insecurities. He will feed your hunger for love with his well-rehearsed plethora of lies.

Pay heed. This kind of man will not leave you standing. He does not get his impeccable reputation from leaving prey alive. He will pound with lightning precision and he will always go ruthlessly for the jugular. Your antidote to this man will be to give him the Rumpelstiltskin prescription. Call him out once and you will never deal with him again. The art of magic is for none to see the trick because once the puppet strings are exposed, the show is over.

The Love Potion continued...

"Hehehe!" Vatete burst out laughing much to my indignation.

"Don't you like it?" I asked, voice trembling slightly disgusted at myself that at my age I still needed her validation.

10

"It is very good for war." She answered. "You young people like to fight, but love is subtle my lovely."

"Vatete, please tell us about the love potion now." Nattu begged

"Yes of course." Vatete cleared her throat leaning forward to un-shell the peanuts which we had given to her with her favorite cup of 5 Roses tea.

"Once upon a time, a long time ago, a young woman just like you and Chi went to the medicine woman of her village and said…"

"My husband grows weary of me. We argue heatedly every day. I would like a love potion to make him fall in love with me again."

"Of course," said the medicine woman. "I can prepare something for you right away." And off she went to prepare the Love Potion of all times. We stared wide eyes wondering if it was really so simple. All we needed was a love potion in lieu of all our *how-to* magazines.

"But before I proceed, read to me from your blog girls. I am sorry if I hurt your feelings with my laughter. It is only wisdom that makes me mirthful over your ignorance and bliss."

"Ok. Vatete. I will read to you some more." I happily grabbed my bedazzled Hello Kitty laptop, proud of the opportunity to impress this mysterious lady with all the secrets on love.

10 Reasons to Die to the Old to Be the Born Again Femme Fatale

CTM

"I used to chase men now I'm chasing my destiny and dreams."

I would love to address love and only the best aspects of it, but it's a cold and harsh world and, oftentimes, all you are left with is a gaping hole where your heart used to be. What are your options? Curl up and die a small death?

This blog is for those women who are at the end of their rope. Love has eluded you and continues to avoid you. Perhaps it's your loose truths, your unbridled ability to love without head games, or the bump on your crooked nose. No matter what the defect is or just an anomaly of fate because naturally you still attest to perfection, it's time to wipe your mascara-ruined face and take your power back.

Here is a toast to all the scavengers of love who are tired of living on the outskirts of what others take for granted... a 'normal love life'. You were destined for far greater things. You are a survivor in training and here are **10 sound reasons why you should die to old to be the born again femme fatale.**

#1 Why is the definition for "Femme Fatale" so harsh?

"An attractive and seductive woman, especially one who will ultimately bring disaster to a man who becomes involved with her."

If you are a man and you bring a woman to ruin, you are patted on the back as an admirable player. After all, it's a man's birthright to build and destroy what he surveys right? Yet when Adam listens to Eve's lies, Samson allows Delilah to cut his hair or David is seduced by Bathsheba taking a moonlight bath, it is the women who are held solely responsible and eternally immortalized as villains.

In every other arena, women are disenfranchised of their power. But when it comes to wrongdoing, they are suddenly supernatural in this ability, compared to men. Consider the witch-hunt of hundreds of women of power and influence like Joan of Arc in 18th Century England. How convenient it was to suddenly decree that it was the right thing to burn this threat on a stake. The demonization of women in relationships is legendary. Women are the 'whores' in society, never men. Yet, in most instances, the skin trade is a position of desperation for women and one of sheer, careless pleasure for men.

Yet women are considered the perpetrators and men their victims.

The way one woman is mistreated is the burden of us all as it will be the inheritance of our daughters, mothers and sisters. The first great price of being a Femme Fatale is that you no longer subscribe to what men and ignorant, mentally-enslaved women think anymore. You have evolved from being merely human to being the sexy, confident superhero of your own life. Welcome to your new empowered self. Now discover your super powers.

#2 A femme fatal is both very beautiful and very intelligent.

This is your first super power. Ladies, I cannot stress the importance of personal development. Spend some time in your local library and reach for something outside of *Vogue* magazine. You will find the greatest love stories in classics like Thomas Hardy's *Far From The Madding Crowd*.

Jane Austen will satisfy your fashion curiosity with the manners and dress sense of an era and Lord Byron and Shakespeare will share with you the many ways a man can adore you. Reading will expand the borders of your mind no matter who you are, or your station in life. Your paper and hardcover journey will never leave you the same.

Beauty is how you see the world and not how it sees you. Beauty alone cannot withstand the test of time, but your intelligence will ride off with you into the sunset of your making.

#3 Your next super power is to cultivate your style.

If you are sexy and curvy, don't squeeze yourself into dresses cut for narrow-hipped girls. A *femme fatale* always embodies the presence of who she truly is. This Goddess dresses for herself not her ex Jimmy or that guy Mike who asked her out for dinner next week. These men are all the microscopic insects of another lifetime. The old you. The new you is bigger than life.

Put on your dazzling peach lipstick, throw on that Bohemian necklace, and lift your head and strut you stuff. Smell like a million dollars. Take care of yourself. Be impeccable in being the best version of you at all times. Cultivate the discipline to do this because it is this quality that is the key to being a *femme fatale* over the very lovely external byproducts of possessing it.

It will be a cold day in hell before a man stops you dead in your tracks again. Let your boots do the talking as you step over anyone or anything in your way. You now understand what true love is. It's loving yourself. Superheroes don't explain or excuse themselves to civilians they just are. They can talk about you in your wake. That is the purpose of the dull minded. Yours is now only to sparkle. Center stage.

#4 A femme fatale is heartless.

Now please don't cringe. I am not the one who tore your heart out. But you won't need it going forth. A heart is a nice placeholder for something better. A heart is susceptible to being hurt. Not having one is your fourth super power. Name calling, betrayal and lies will be water off a ducks back. Who cares? You have no tears to cry.

You have a soul of steel. You are an advocate for the poor, a defender of the weak and a lethal weapon of mass destruction for any fool weak enough to wander into your domain. Never ask for love. Never profess yours and never share your truths. All these things are your kryptonite. The new you is invincible. You are in pursuit of nothing.

You seek to wash your make off after a successful day at work and have a sound night of sleep. Trust no one and remember sex is overrated. Where men are concerned, promise nothing and deliver the same. After all, you will be at fault in the end no matter what is done to you. So keep your hands clean. If he wants to lust after you give him enough rope to hang himself. It's hardly your concern. Trust me, it will still be on your tab. But you can afford to pay it. In full.

#5 A femme fatale is always graceful under fire.
You must expect to be hated and attacked. We live in a fear-ridden world and like a writer once said, 'You are either busy living or busy dying.' People who are busy dying want a cold body next to them in their shallow, self-made graves of hell. Your new super power is that you understand human nature.

You smell the BS from a trillion miles away. You hear the envy with your bionic ears and you sense when a situation or person will be to your benefit or detriment. These are your fifth set of superpowers. Even in the movies the pre-hero person is suddenly subject to something which is supposed to destroy them, but instead makes them stronger. Cat-woman is my favorite antihero. She is perfectly flawed. Very human. But it takes nothing from her extra-ordinary abilities.

#6 Expect nothing, but pray for everything.
It is impossible to push someone who is lying on their back. It is equally impossible to disappoint someone who expects nothing or hurt someone who has no feelings on the table. I strongly advise you take all necessary precautions to amputate anything which would be a weakness.

I am an African woman and I have been called the N word more times than I can remember by people whom I thought I could trust. This is the sixth superpower you will need. Discharge words of their power against you. Identify your buttons and why they exist and disarm them.

When people call me the N word I love it. It shows me who they really are. It proves to me that I am so intimidating that they are reaching. It thrills me to smile and have no energy response to it because that is the moment that they see my cape and realize that I am indeed larger than life. Words are like a gun pointed at the one using them. Other people's words are not your problem. How you respond is yours.

#7 A femme fatale is mysterious.
Save your childhood stories for therapy. No one truly cares. People have their own crosses to bear. Forget trying to be understood. People will misconstrue you at will and take you out of context at the drop of a pin. It doesn't matter if you have only shown them kindness, respect and honesty. They will decapitate you without hesitation and without batting an eyelid.

In life there are two kinds of people. Prey and predators. Be a predator. Be vague. Refuse to have your privacy invaded and fiercely guard your secrets. Let them eat their hearts out, rather than yours because they are only out to hurt you with yourself and nothing more.

#8 Have a bloody sense of humor.
Life is a stage with its fair share of fools, jesters and jugglers. See the entertainment value in things. Laugh until your belly aches and your eyes tear up. Surround yourself with people you adore, who adore you. The rest are window gazers. There are no court-side tickets to your life for the peanut gallery.

#9 Don't let a man determine your value.
You call the shots over you. If he thinks you are damaged goods, let him go? You have nothing to prove to anyone. A femme fatale is an Alpha woman — the most dangerous of her species. Act like a leader of the pack. Speak with

calculated delivery. Take your time to read people and seek to understand what makes them tick. Be kind to those who require it.

A true femme fatale is a class act and a lady, but she will never let any man, woman or organization walk all over her. All these things add up to extremely high intricate value. This is your ninth superpower.

#10 Last but not least, burn this blog and make your own rules.
A true femme fatale charters her own path in life. Only you know the things which bind you and the ties you must break. It's your call to speak up when something is wrong and to be of service to those less equipped than you. A true femme fatale wants her tribe to have her back, but does not need anybody. The least of all is a mere man.

There are rules of engagement in this life and failure to know and understand them is not an excuse from their repercussions. Not understanding gravity will not prevent you from falling to your death. A true femme fatale is her superhero version of her natural self. You will need to cultivate all your talents and operate at your full potential. You cannot be superhero dependent on other people to conquer life.

Unlike the popular context, being a femme fatale is neither about hating men nor trying to seduce them. It's all about you. It's about not caring about anyone who doesn't care for you. It's about being very discerning and picky of those who claim they do. Being a femme fatale is the *national anthem* of every single mother, every divorced woman, abandoned woman, widow, orphan, married woman, girlfriend, lover or nun.

This woman is Alpha. She understands what men don't need permission in blogs to grasp that it's her life and she is going to live it her way.

The Love Potion continued...

"I like this one," said Vatete with a smile. "Indeed, every woman must understand her power and then a good woman will pick to use this power for good."

"Please tell us more about love potions Vatete this blog is not as exciting as that." Nattu playfully jabbed me in the side with her elbow.

"After many hours, the old woman re-entered the hut holding a small glass bottle with white powder in it and a green river pebble." Vatete continued her story. "You must memorize the instructions which I am about to give you because if you make one wrong turn, I fear your love is lost."

Nattu and I gasped out loud, hearts pounding and sweaty palms.

"What happened next?" we both asked spell bound by her intriguing story.

"Patience girls, patience. Mmmmh. We can start your lesson in patience. Read me more of your American blog," she tossed a handful of peanuts into her mouth and begin chewing them with a crunchy rhythm.

"Patience is so boring. I would rather do the love potion lesson Tete," I sulked.

"Well then, we will need to spend more time teaching you that lesson Chi because the lessons which you would most escape are the ones that you need the most."

Super Skinny at the Very Top!
10 Steps That Will Make You an Instant Size O

"You may be whatever dress size you feel sexy in, and can rock as long as you have a size 0 personality," he insisted.

In this world of anorexic dreams that are starved of hope due to the prevailing economic hardships worldwide, everyone is a glutton of worry. The emotional, spiritual, mental, and physical baggage that most of us are lugging around is not designer, but is certainly in by design.

How heavy you are is the first thing that others notice about you, especially when embarking into a new relationship. The weight of our souls need not be weighed by a fancy bathroom scale, but by a more fine-tuned and sophisticated instrument that is inherent to us all – our intuition. We all know people who have a 'heavy' energy. They rarely smile, they take a lot of coaxing to be happy, never laugh out loud and, after we spend time with them, no matter how much we love them, we feel exhausted and drained. These are the obsessive consumers of all things unhealthy, like fear based news, conspiracy theorists and naysayers with a very bleak expectation of the future.

Everybody wants to date someone skinny with a ready smile, a light and bubbly energy, lots of funny jokes and good stories and always looking at the things on the bright side. This is the most important diet which you will ever go on in your life. Here are 10 fast steps that will make you an instant size 0 personality!

#1 Join the gym! After years of feeding your mind with greasy thoughts and your ears with uncensored junk food, it is time to clean up your act! This will require more than sitting at home and reading this article. You will have to get up off your behind and find a place that is equipped to get you back into tip-top shape. For some, this might be a church or a temple, for others it might be a Tony Robbins Seminar, and still for others it might be a cool AA meeting.

No matter which place you pick, we all have that one place we gravitate towards when it is time to make things right. Go! This is an environment that has been set up to give you access to all the equipment that you need to turn that over weight-depressed personality into a stunning size 0!

#2 Begin a balanced diet! We are what we eat, so no matter how hard you work out, you will only start to get real and lasting results when you change your diet. Reprogram your cable settings to TV shows that are uplifting and inspiring to you, and watch news shows that keep you updated with world politics without digging you into a dejected pit. Get some tapes of your favorite music to play in your car, or even go ahead and buy those cheesy positive reaffirmation tapes. Go see a play, go listen to the latest jazz band, just fill all your free spaces with fun!

The hardest thing is going to be flushing your system of old negative acquaintances and low-energy friends. If you can, simply change your phone number. If not, just don't feed into their negativity. Quickly change the subject, and for everything negative they say, find five positive things and watch them turn and go. It is true that misery loves company, and you are no longer the hostess of the world's best pity party!

#3 An apple a day. Although it might seem silly at first, make it a must to put something healthy into your system daily. Get your phone to text you a motivational line a day, or put out visualization boards that you made over a bottle of champs with all the cool places in the world you'd like to see. Whatever it is, access it daily to take place of all the not-so-pleasant toxic worry you've been carrying around with you since this recession started!

#4 No carbs! No matter how bored you are, do not go back to your old friends and ways! Instead, make it a point to have a long list of things you want to do. The thought of wasting any more of your God-given time is insane to you! Don't even cheat in the middle of the night by responding to the late night booty call, as it will have you plummeting back to the valley of depression and regret. It sucks starting any diet over!

#5 Emotional cardio is the sweaty, tedious and very difficult act of looking long and hard at yourself and what you need to work on and improve. Yes, the economy is going to shit. Yes, our troops need to come back home. But stop finding faults within the world and find what's wrong with you. Make a list and immediately go to work on improving those things! Were you broke anyway before this recession because you dropped out of school? Go back to a community college and take a class. Do you have an anger problem that will hinder you from being an employee of the month when you finally get the job flipping burgers? Take an anger management class! The world moves at such a fast pace that when you are blessed with an opportunity when things slow down ... well, that's your chance to get back on the horse and get ready to hit the ground running.

#6 No diet pills! There are no quick-fix diets that really work and are truly good for your health. So buckle down, pace yourself and stay committed and focused. You won't achieve everything in a day, but the moment you begin you are already a size 0!

#7 Boot camp is always an option if you want to see quick results. Do all of the above and immediately begin surrounding yourself with good people who are motivated and uplifting. Share your dietary goals with them and watch them, and the universe will whip you back to the best stage of your life.

#8 A personal trainer. Approach someone you trust and respect and solicit their support. You will have an emotional accountability partner who will remind you that whom you aspire to become is a sight better than the bitch or asshole you have become. Being around them and looking at their stunning size 0 personality, will also remind you why you are even going through all this hard work and keeping to your diet diligently!

#9 Lifting weights basically involves lifting your own weight in the community around you and doing your fair share of charity work. There's nothing like giving back at a local orphanage for the afternoon to lose those selfish emotional calories and drop a lot of weight in just one day. Glance at yourself in the mirror … now who knew!

#10 The skinny girls club is very exclusive, and not just any heavy broad can join it. But once you've put in your work and got your membership card, watch your life change overnight! This club is home to some of the most amazing, accomplished, kind, compassionate and beautiful people that you will ever meet. They will take you under their wings because you have a size 0 personality and open doors which you never even dreamed existed for you and usher you in.

Money, outer beauty and power cannot get you into this club no matter how hard you try. Only your stunning perfect size 0 personality can. Smile, hold your head up high and raise your skinny bitch martini glass because baby, it's super skinny at the very top!

The Love Potion continued…

"First you are to awaken at the earliest crack of dawn. You must be the first young woman down by the river bathing in the first light of dawn. In the evening you must be the last bathing in the golden light of dusk," Vatete told us with an earnest tone of voice.

"Well I'm not a morning person so goes that prescription out the door." Nattu mumbled under her breath.

"No. No. No. You must both train to wake up at the crack of dawn. This is the nature of this love potion my girls."

"Yes Vatete we understand." We smiled at her benevolently.

24

"Mmmmmh. I hope you do my darlings because I do not understand this size zero blog. Remember what is good for a man's touch is not what is good for the hands. We will learn this more advanced lesson on a different day.

For now, I must hear more of what today's young woman thinks about love and then I will continue to tell you more about the best love potion in the world."

Snow White and the Seven Dwarfs! 10 Reasons Why Some of Your BFF'S Should Be Men!

Above: A picture of Snow White and the Seven Dwarfs. *Credit:* 'Snow White and the Seven Dwarfs' movie

"Come. You Have A Home With Us!" Said the Seven Dwarfs.

The all too familiar scene! Poor little Snow White lost in a concrete jungle. Haters want your heart served on a silver plate. Debts men have sent the huntsman to collect at all costs. The word is out on the streets you're a wanted woman, but not by men. You feel sad and alone, but don't be in despair. Find the seven dwarfs and they'll help keep you happy, busy, entertained and on ice. Until Prince Charming melts you with a kiss.

Here are 10 fabulous reasons Why Some of Your Best Friends Should Be Men.

#1 Meet Grumpy! We all have a Grumpy in our lives. When it's hot, it's too hot. When it's cold, it's too darn cold. When the real estate market was booming, houses were too expensive. Now it's crashed he's going to wait for it to keep crashing before he can commit. Whether it's Bush or Obama in office, the government sucks. No matter how hard you try to make him smile, he'd rather peer at you suspiciously for being too nice and keep frowning.

Don't hate on Grumpy. He is always there for a great pity party. Grumpy always has your sobbing knife-stabbed back. Appreciate him as a good friend and an example of everything you don't want in a man. His advice can be biting, but always honest. Seriously this pessimistic naysayer is a girl's secret best friend.

#2 Meet Dopey! Every girl needs Dopey in her life. He is usually a surfer dude type who doesn't take life too seriously. He'd rather hit the surf than hit on you. He is never short of 420 if you need it. He thinks all dudes are cool, so that will keep your perspective balanced and your personality cool and dope. Dopey might seem mellow, but you will need more than a set of D cups to hang out with him. He will playfully point out things about yourself you could work on. Take notes. Resist the urge to make him your rebound guy and you'll have a friend for life.

#3 Meet Happy! Happy is ironically very annoying. He is that guy friend who never seems to have bad day. It's all about good energy and positive thinking. After the decade you've had, you could certainly use some cheering up. He will never loan you any cash and if he reluctantly does, you'll never hear the end of it even after you pay him back. He will send you daily postings of your dream job and connect you to good people. No matter how mopey you are, he will always make you laugh.

Happy is a decent, hardworking guy, but just not your type. He sticks around half hoping things will someday turn romantic. He asked you out once and you turned him down and it didn't even faze him. If he asks you out again, tell him no with a smile. Remind him to have a positive attitude towards it. To even have a one night stand with Happy would ruin your friendship. Trust me, he is a much better friend than a boyfriend.

#4 Meet Sneezy! Sneezy is loud and uncouth and you wish you'd run into that girl who stole your ex hanging out with him. Sneezy can be ultra-feminine or gay and that's what makes him one of the most coveted guy friends of the seven. He understands how you feel. He will spend the day shopping and even though he is bitchier than you... who cares! Sneezy at best will help you with your hair, make-up and styling. Don't worry if he dates hotter guys than you. Just focus on healing your broken heart and learning to be sassy. A friendship with Sneezy will make you outspoken and confident.

#5 Meet Sleepy! He is not your trendiest buddy, but so what. He never reads the paper or watches TV. His days seem to involve work and sleep only. All his spare time is spent with you. Sleepy is an accomplished homebody who will teach you to love being at home. He will teach you to cook and get you candles and bubble bath and insist you take hour long soaks.

Sleepy doesn't care what you look like dressed up. He is more likely to admire an old pair of sweats. Just don't spend time with him at his place alone. Better to call him. He is always home and pleased to listen to you vent for hours giving great advise.

#6 Meet Doc! You admire what he does for work. He always gives you invaluable advice. His life is on the straight and narrow and it just reminds you that when you decide to focus, all will be well. Doc, overall, thinks of himself as better than anyone else in your life, don't correct him. He is a better problem-solver when he has no competition. Of course you'd never date someone so self-involved but, as a friend, that's great! He is so into himself, you never have to worry about him being into you. He loves to listen to the sound of his own voice, so ask pointed questions then let him do all the talking.

To prevent him from liking you, remind him of all your faults and watch his perfectionist self retreat. Doc will be able to come up with a comprehensive game plan for your life for the next five years. If you take his advice, you'll be better off in the future.

#7 Meet Bashful! Bashful teaches you to like dudes again. He is super sweet and so gorgeous, but usually taken. He'd never cheat on his girl and that just makes him hotter. He likes you as a person and is genuinely concerned about your affairs. He is not a gossip, so you can trust him with all your dirty laundry. He lives vicariously through you, so don't spare him the details of your messy love life.

He can think like a bad boy and has no qualms decoding the bro code for you. He reminds you of all that can be tender, kind and endearing about a man. Bashful is an accessory friend who looks good at any event when you need a hot date. Your friends will all think you are insane not to date him, but you know better. Be very good to him, this guy is priceless.

#8 Meet The Huntsman! The odds are slim, but if you can convince the huntsman that you are a good person, he will work for you not against you. Confront him head on. If it's money owed, be honest and make a realistic proposal for repayment. Do not avoid him because he is trained to hunt you down. If you go to him and are accessible, he will seize to harass you and become a worthy ally. Put his knowledge to use because it's his business to resolve the situation. Between all your great guy friends and the huntsman, you haven't even had time to wonder about Charming's approximate time of arrival.

#9 Meet The Evil Witch! Any girls trying to come into your life after the fact with a bright red apple of friendship should be avoided at all costs. Where were they when you really needed them? No thanks. It is more constructive for you to do something sweet for the seven. Imagine where you would be without them.

#10 Meet Prince Charming! Well, of course, there is a happy ending! Snow White upon meeting the seven dwarfs and eluding the huntsman lives out her wonderful life for many a seasons in the city of angels. Snow is busy, productive and very content. It goes without saying that she catches the eye of a handsome prince. Of course the prince must earn the approval of all of the seven dwarfs because, after all, only they truly have Snow's best interests at heart. With a single kiss, Snow melts. She rides off into the rest of her life, but she never forgets the seven dwarfs nor deletes their numbers from her phone book.

The Love Potion continued...

"Aunty what do you think?" I asked her eagerly.

"Well, in our culture, a young woman must not be seen to be keeping the company of many men," Vatete answered honesty. "But some ways are of the old world. It is indeed advisable to befriend some men to understand what values mean the most to you as long as your meetings are chaperoned with friends.

I chuckled to myself imaging what any one of my BFF's would think of being asked to chaperone me on an outing.

"Well unless you are both ready for bed, I can continue with my story," Vatate teased us with a smile.

"Please!" we both cried.

"Well, the next instruction that the old woman gave that young girl was that she was to sweep the floor in her hut and outside around her hut in the early hours of the morning before her beloved awoke and to sprinkle some more of this love potion all around their home."

"Wow." We both responded.

"She was to repeat this action late in the evening before he returned home as well," continued Vatete. "Now let me rest a while girls. Why don't you ask me any questions about anything which you might have?"

"Do you think that it is possible for a man to remain faithful to a woman Vatete?" Nattu asked

"Well these are some of the thoughts that my girlfriends and I have on it Tete. We wrote them down here."

Monogamous Relationships... Love at Gun Point!
10 Ways to Back Out of an Emotional Corner

"Freeze!" she screamed. "You're under arrest! Put your heart up where I can see it, and slowly step away from other women . . ."

Monogamy is the practice or condition of having one sexual partner at a time. It is also defined as the practice of marrying only once in a lifetime. For those who subscribe to this kind of relationship, your subscription has just been suspended until you understand what monogamy is not. This is not the practice of backing your partner up into a tight emotional corner at gun point and demanding that their entire existence now entirely rotates around you. It is not the practice of now having a single-tracked mind.

"Where is he?" "What is he doing?" and "With whom is he doing it?" It is not the condition whereby you shall be allowed to have only one friend for the rest of your life. It is not the act of leading your partner slowly down the aisle under duress using guilt trips, anger, begging and coaxing to get him to renounce the entire female population and forever only look and be with you.

The only thing that can come out of backing your man into a "right angle" is a wrong result. Love at gun point is a lot of stressful work and a waste of your time and life. To play jail guard to a grown-ass man is the worst job on the planet. So slowly lower your handheld weapon and move aside. Let him out of the place between a rock and your hard, hot head that you have put him in. Only animals live in cages, and even that is something that some animal activists might dispute. This is a man.

Now the question is, is he your man? If he is, he will love you without the wicked threat of getting his brains splattered on the wall. If he is not, then why are you selling yourself short? You have your back to the love of your life who will not even look your way during this emotional highway robbery. Whether he leaves or stays, you win, so here are 10 for-sure ways to back him out of that emotional corner.

#1 Lower your weapon! ... and depending on how long you've had the poor guy's back up against the wall, we will try to figure out if there is any way in hell he will ever trust you again or want to stay. The problem with treating someone like a criminal is that they begin to act like one. It's like sentencing an innocent man to prison. God only knows, but he probably learned a trick or two to avoid upsetting your crazy ass, and he is probably an escape artist when it comes to taking the much-needed time to himself. Lowering your weapon, however, is only the first step. It is a sexy sign of surrender that shows that you are now ready to find true love.

#2 Stand aside and set him free. You will have to eat some humble pie during this process and let him know the truth. You have been so wrong to have a gun to his head, and you are no longer interested in being his jail guard. You obviously have trust issues, but justified or not, no person has the right to consume the life of another.

Our unalienable rights are individual and uncompromising. In my country and Shona culture, we have a saying that, 'Once a goat has been tied to a tree for a long time, when the rope has been cut off, the goat will still keep going around the tree for a while before it realizes it is free.' You must realize that this is not a healthy relationship, so there will be emotional trauma on both sides. Talk it out to give your relationship a real chance of coming out of this dusty corner.

#3 Unload the gun and put it away! Do not leave the gun lying around loaded. Remember, you are hard wired to use it and you are still at risk of shooting to kill. So unload the gun and put it in a safe place. This refers to unloading your mind and heart of all suspicious and negative thoughts and creating new thought patterns. Instead of 'What is he doing?' ask 'What am I doing?' Instead of asking, 'Where is he going?' ask 'Where am I going?' Instead of asking, 'Who is he with?' ask 'Who am I?'.

#4 Find circles in your corners. Corners are finite and circles are infinite. Corners are restrictive and circles exploratory. Corners are for individuals and circles can encompass a couple. Corners are conclusive, but circles are open yet safely closed. Corners are temporary, but circles are for an eternity. Which do you choose?

#5 Find a brand new occupation! So now that you are no longer in the business of stealing hearts by force, whatever shall you do with your pretty self? Go back to the chalkboard. Before you met him, what made you happy? What did you love to do? How did you spend your time? Find what makes you tick. Find what makes you feel warm inside. Even better, find something you love equally or even more than you love him ... that isn't another man, of course.

#6 Mutual attraction is as obvious as the time on a clock. So are you both half past anger and a quarter to love? Or half past love and a quarter to moving on? Either way, deal with it. If you can bear labor to have a beautiful child, you can push through this to find the relationship of your dreams. Is he still into you? Is he making an effort? Is he forgiving, loving, supportive and proud of you for the new direction in your life? Only you know the answers to these questions.

#7 Mutual distractions are really healthy in a monogamous relationship if you should both decide to stay together. Someone once said, 'Let there be spaces in your togetherness.' Instead of panicking and feeling like your lover will slip away, think of those spaces as vital pockets of oxygen. Monogamous relationships are a deep sea dive into the unknown, and trust you are going to need all the oxygen you can get to keep breathing and stay alive.

#8 The role of dream catcher is much more desirable for you. What are your dreams as a couple and how are you going to achieve them? Women have the innate gift of resourcefulness and creativity which is God-given. You would be surprised what a single mom can whip up in the kitchen for her kids on limited supplies or a young woman in the bedroom on all sorts of supplies for her lover. Take that talent and apply it to creating a value system in your relationship where your partner values your ideas and input. Get to the point where you regard your guy as your emotional partner, not your prisoner. Prisoners escape, but partners stay together.

#9 Freeze! You are under arrest! Is now only something you will say if you work for the Police Department? Otherwise, if you want to be loved and to love, be patient. Forcing things with the catalyst of desperation will only lead into a hellhole of a relationship. It is easier to do things right the first time than to correct a bad situation. So don't be in a rush to get to the end of your new monogamous relationship.

#10 While you were out catching up with old friends, he missed you! When you were out running, you got your figure and your honey back. When you were too busy trusting him to sweat him on the small stuff, you rediscovered your passion and he rediscovered the woman that he fell in love with. Now isn't love a silly thing!

The Love Potion continued...

"Well firstly to answer your question on monogamy before I continue with my story..." Vatete paused. "All things are in equal proportions possible and impossible."

We both nodded knowing this instinctively to be the truth.

"Where monogamy is possible, a young woman must almost aid love along its way with..."

"A secret love potion!" We both exclaimed, thinking we understood everything but understanding nothing.

36

"Vatete, you must finish the story since this love potion seems to be the cure all our romantic mishaps." We both sighed.

"Yes, with pleasure girls. So back to the village of Maputi, the next instruction which you must write on your heart is concerning food," said the old woman. "And perhaps this one is the most important of all."

"I never cook Vatete, but I know how to cook. I just get busy and prefer to eat out." I interrupted excitedly.

"Qeqeqeqeqe" Vatete clicked her tongue shaking her head in disapproval. "Firstly, you must learn to hold your tongue Chi! Secondly, in this story young lady, the old woman tells the young married girl that she must prepare her husband's favorite meal three times a day and sprinkle it with a pinch full of the love potion."

"You'd never make it Chi. I don't think burnt boiled eggs count!" Nattu threw herself on the cloud of pillows behind her, rolling over with belly laughter.

"Well then I can just be a gold digger and marry a rich man and someone else can prepare the meal for me," I said poking out my tongue in jest. "Speaking of which I think I wrote something on that. Vatete you will surely approve!"

"You girls have much to learn, but that is why I am here." She smiled nodding her head in permission.

Gold Digging 101
Will You Strike Gold During The
Recession? 10 Quick Tricks!

CTM

"Showing you his leased-out Bent sure won't pay your rent!" she laughed wholeheartedly.

Welcome dudes and dolls to Gold Digging 101! The only course prerequisite is the presence of a pulse and the absence of morals and integrity! Let's begin!

What makes smart, sexy, beautiful girls become gold diggers? The Blue Stocking Society of 1750 of course! An informal social and educational movement for women that advocated for the displacement of traditional gender roles and promoted equality in the work place, the Blue Stocking movement is singularly one of the most influential factors to Cinderella having to go back to find work at her step mother's house.

Modern society for today's women is the arena of the most baffling catch 22 of this century. You are either an over-worked and under-appreciated superwoman with both a high-powered career and a suburban bliss home life, an all-career socially ostracized woman piling up her financial nest eggs as your biological nest eggs wither up and dry, or the secretly pitied stay-at-home underdog mom with hypocritical friends who always tell you that being a mom is the most important job in the world, but also believe that you are missing out on living in the 21st century.

So what is the answer? Well, here are 10 quick tricks that you will need to know if you choose the role of gold digger!

#1 Only fools rush in! In LaLa Land, just about every other guy looks like a gold mine worth digging! Hold your horses! Chances are, any guy sitting at the dinner table having a million dollars transferred into his private off-shore bank account is also having a hundred silly girls transferred to his bed and certainly a million little micro germs and potential diseases transferred to you! Yuck! Put your shovel away for another day, enjoy dinner and hope that his credit card doesn't get rejected.

#2 Gold Digging is a Partnership between digger and *diggee*. Shovels are tough and they hit the ground hard, so I refuse to feel sorry for any guy sitting sniffling in the corner crying over how some gold digger took him for all he is worth without his knowledge. Really?! Or is the truth that like a magpie attracted to a shiny trinket, you ran into aluminum foil thinking that is was silver you could steal with nobody looking?

If you're exploiting someone, expect to be exploited right back. You are digging into bodies you shouldn't be, and they are digging into pockets they shouldn't be. So guys, quit having your cake, eating it and then complaining about it! Just move out of the dessert area because you just might end up with a toothache!

#3 Good girls always wear their hard hats! No miner in her right mind would climb into an unpredictable underground mine without a hard hat! For all the name calling, stone throwing and near public lynching that you are going to face in your new role, you are going to need very tough skin and a very hard hat! Although your choice of profession might already be indicative of extensive, irreparable brain damage — in which case wear the hat only because it looks cute. The life of a gold digger is a lonely path. Live by the shovel ... be buried by one.

#4 Keep looking at his shoes and you'll trip. Scuffed up shoes don't make a bum and good shoes don't make a baller player. Rather, watch how he walks — not his natural swagger and his bling-bling Rolex — but his mannerisms and his actions. Withholding a dollar bill from a waitress who has bent over backwards to make your dining experience enchanting is ugly, and ignoring the valet guy holding out keys to a brand new Porsche is scandalous. Trust that if he can't honor those who serve his stomach, you'll also be out on your ass with the trash before morning. At least the trash has a ride to the dumpster!

#5 The gold rush is not a pretty sight! Girls of all shapes and sizes are breaking a sweat (and their heels) in an effort to catch a glimpse of some so-called rich guy. People's feelings get trampled on during a gold rush, entire friendships are lost and any potential relationships with really great guys are forfeited. In the shanty town which will now be your new not-so-glamorous digs, camping out the best years of your life on the outskirts of some rich guy's life, expect the following: vicious gossip, negativity-polluted air, unsanitary sex, corrupt intimacy and a breeding ground of brothel-like affections of jaded women who are an easy prey for lone wolves.

#6 She who digs last digs deepest! As with most good things in life, gold mines included, by the time that you, your mamma and your mamma's mamma hear about it, it's a done deal! Most guys only need to have money at only one point in their lives, and they will gladly have women around them trying to dig for more for than the rest of theirs! It's going to take more work than you bargained for when you are digging an old, used-up mine.

Chances are, you will hit a big, hard rock of a man who has been so abused by life that his only mission now is to make yours as miserable as he can manage. There is no shame in hanging up your shovel and walking away.

#7 Beware the leprechaun! Birds of a feather flock together. If you are a gold digger, chances are your friends are, too! Surely, you of all people know that they certainly can't be trusted — not with your friendship, your wallet or your man!

You might be lucky enough to find that pot of gold at the end of the rainbow, but good luck holding onto it.

#8 Gold diggers have babies, too! Have you ever tried to plough a field with a fussy, irritable baby tied to your back?

You might want to practice, because trying to hold a shovel, elbow your way through a gold rush and dig for gold with a baby is going to take every ounce of strength you've got!

41

#9 So what's the point?! Exactly! Congratulations on successfully completing your course! You now have a brain. A good head on your shoulders and some gray matter are going to be your prerequisites for the finals.

#10 Gold is a natural resource! If you truly want to be the best gold digger in the world, it's simple! Look for the natural talent in a man. Find what makes him dream. What are his goals and ambitions?

If you are lucky enough to strike gold and find a good man who is willing to work his ass off for you and his babies for the rest of both your lives, then stand proudly by his side because you have truly struck it rich! For a lifetime of happiness, peace and of course prosperity!

The Love Potion continued...

"Yes indeed this is a good lesson my dear. Nattu, what is the moral of this blog?" Vatete asked Nattu

"The moral here Tete is that there is more to a good man than his money. In fact, this is often a trap," chimed in Nattu

"And..." I interrupted. "It is far wiser to pick someone with whom you share a certain affinity and who possesses equal potential and ambition to be a life partner."

"Excellent!" praised Vatete "Mhandara dzakura!"

"That means we are now mature young ladies in case you forgot all your Shona living your fancy Beverly Hills lifestyle," Nattu teased me pulling at my braids.

"Ok back to the juicy love potion story Vatete so what happened next?" I asked

42

"I would hope some of the instructions were for the young girl to wash her face so that she would appear more beautiful to her husband?" Nattu asked

Vatete threw her head back revealing the charming gap in between her front teeth which was the signature for beauty of women of my Shona tribe, Vayera Soko.

"Perhaps you can share with me your thoughts on this before I continue with my story..."

Extreme Make Over To Make You Perfect!
10 Things to Nip & Tuck!

"So, tell me what you don't like about yourself?" they asked.

Pursuit of perfection is the holy grail of modern times. Plastic surgery is the magic wand that promises to turn Helen the troll into Helen of Troy. The ugly truth behind this is simple: it is the attainment of power. Beauty is synonymous to power in today's culture and is cultishly revered.

It is worshiped on the silver screen, on the covers of glossy magazines and on every glittering city billboard. It is impossible to escape the spell cast by a beautiful face, even with the full realization that it is merely bait with a catch, especially in the unscrupulous world of entertainment and advertising.

In its purest form, beauty can be used to move and to inspire others to greatness. In its lowest incarnation, it is a wicked tool of deception and of manipulation. Even as highly acclaimed stocks plummet and the global economic markets crash, the value of beauty will never depreciate.

In conjunction with the pursuit of eternal youth, we will continue in our endless pursuit of an elusive beauty. So here are 10 hot tips on thing to nip and tuck so that you can be perfect!

#1 **Nose Job**. There is absolutely no escaping the fact that your nose is one of the first things that people see, and if it is extremely large, there is no going around it. One's nose determines how everything else falls into place on one's face and, therefore, to want to fix this glaring detail is smart.

In relationships, the Pinocchio Syndrome is the first thing that you notice about others and them about you. The bigger the lie, the longer the nose. It is impossible to overlook a blatant lie staring you in the face. Over time, half-truths and white lies begin the take their toll on the entire face of the relationship, and it is time for a major makeover! Learning to be honest comes from knowing and having confidence in what one wants and then demanding it from those in their lives. It's simple.

Once our dreams and goals are clearly defined, we only need to deal with those people who support and facilitate us to achieve them. In love, we must have a clearly defined agenda. Honest and clear articulation of our expectations of others helps us to find happiness as we begin to attract only what we desire and to repel the rest.

45

It is impossible to ever be a stunning beauty with a messed up nose, so ditch the Pinocchio Syndrome, cut out the BS and see everything in your love life and life transform because of your stunning new nose job.

#2 Boob job. The most popular of all cosmetic surgeries would have to be the boob job. Naturally, taste is subjective, but it is easy to understand the attraction to identically large breasts, especially in tight clothes. In LA, the self-proclaimed home of beauties with boobies, girls leading with their chests are a dime a dozen. The augmentation of personality is a lot less expensive and a lot more effective.

Leading with personality is a great way to get noticed in a sea of brainless mannequins. Sure, they look good. So does the well-dressed doll in the window of Louis Vuitton, but no-one is clamoring to take it home and introduce it to one's friends and family. So take out your surgical tools (a pen and paper) and write down all the things that you and others don't like about yourself.

Are you short-tempered, moody, whiny? Whatever your faults are, being aware of them is the first step to making the necessary adjustments. Without being too hard on yourself, actively engage in the act of improving yourself. Read books, join support groups, go to therapy, and talk it out. Do whatever works best for you to begin on drilling these things out of your system. And, as with most things, practice makes perfect!#

#3 Lip job. Lips are a very sensual and essential part of our bodies. Having nice, full lips is very attractive as it draws kisses. Women spend insane amounts of money injecting their lips to achieve fullness in a process that is both painful and oftentimes disastrous. It would make more sense to spend time working on what comes out of one's mouth. Words are powerful weapons that are carelessly used to nuke on a daily basis.

In a relationship, words can be used to soothe, seduce, entertain, abuse or hurt. It is so important to think of the desired result before speaking. If you need to lie, then you are not with the right person.

If you are in love with someone, you should find yourself picking only the bright, gorgeous vivid colors from your palette to paint a wonderful masterpiece. With words, you can conjure up what you visualize in your mind's eye. So go ahead — dream big and speak out loud!

#4 Eye job. Poets have said that eyes are the windows to the soul. Small, beady eyes are very different from wide-open eyes. It is very unattractive to have dirty, small windows to one's soul through which no one can look. We are all attracted to wide open innocence. It is for this very reason that there is a surgical procedure in which the eyes are opened up to look bigger.

In relationships, we all want to be with someone who we believe has good vision. They see us for whom we are, and they can also look into the future and see and support us for who we would like to become. If you are dating someone blind, you are selling yourself short.

If you are walking around with your eyes closed, your needs not met or treated badly, then open them. The world is a magical, beautiful place with many opportunities. So don't waste your life living with your eyes closed. The gift of true vision is priceless.

#5 Facelift. Over time, life happens and there is no shame in wanting to rewind the hands of the clock. A really good facelift can freshen up the general appearance of an individual. It is prudent to assume that our relationships require the same attention. Stopping to take inventory and look really close up in the mirror is wise.

Switch up your hair, make-up or the way you dress. Break up the routine you've settled into as a couple (or even as a single person) and do something different.

Keeping things fresh is a good way to tap into your youthful spirit of uninhibited adventure, which is exceptionally attractive and will draw others to you for friendship and for love.

#6 Brazilian butt lift. We all have junk in our trunks and things that won't quit following us around! Our behinds are as much a part of us as our present and our future. The trick is keeping trim and firm. Allowing one's past to drag them down is like letting gravity do away with what God blessed you with in your booty department.

Someone with a firm grip on past events is a very attractive partner. It's pointless trying to escape the past, but shedding as much of its weight as is possible is a really good idea. A nice, well-defined behind is an asset. So is someone who accepts all things, good and bad, that have occurred in the past and is gracious and learns from them and moves on.

#7 Tummy tuck. It's hard to look cute with a big belly that is super out of proportion to the rest of one's body. A tummy tuck is the fastest way to do away with that and look instantly slimmer. Any obsessive behaviors that give way to a fat belly are something to be mercilessly amputated from one's life. Don't think twice. Don't flinch. Just stop it.

#8 Cheek Implants are used to accentuate the face. After working on so much and really loving yourself, it's time to show off! What are the unique little quirks that make you special? Your charm, your wit, your humor ... flaunt it!

48

#9 Hand job? Get your mind out of the gutter! The next innovative surgery which I would like to see is hand jobs. There are one too many women going around with the faces of twenty year olds and the hands of ninety year olds. To think you are perfect and beautiful and to not give back in some way, shape or form is wrong. Only through generosity and kindness may one truly elevate themselves onto a pedestal from which others may admire them.

#10 Body contouring is an overall nip and tuck that makes sure the entire body looks hot. An extreme makeover is the only way to become extremely attractive overnight.

The Love Potion continued...

"Ah... I see the wisdom here," said Vatete. "Much like in my story if you can pay attention long enough to hear the end of it."

We all giggled, slapping open palms as is a customary communication of camaraderie in my Shona culture.

"Well back to the village of Maputi," said Vatete, rocking back and forth. "It was the rainy season and as the clouds gathered on the horizon, dark and moody. The old woman handed the young woman an animal skin made bag with the secret love potion in it."

We both nodded, speechless.

"Do you remember all the instructions which I have given you?" asked the old woman

"Yes, I do." Answered the young woman. "I am to get up at the crack of dawn and go down to the river and bath. I am also supposed to bath before the last light of day with this love potion."

The old woman grunted tossing little twigs into the crackling fire.

"Then I am to sweep twice inside and around my hut at the crack of dawn and late at night and both times I am the sprinkle a pinch of the love potion all around."

"Indeed," crooned the old woman.

"And the most important of these is that I am to prepare my husband's favorite meal up to thrice a day and put a pinch of this love potion in it each time."

The young woman smiled knowing that she had understood the instructions well.

"I forgot one more instruction..." the old woman sniffed some tobacco. "Whenever you are upset and you have harsh words to say to your husband, put this green river pebble in your water and wash your mouth with water and spit the water out. You must remain silent for an entire hour after this action for the love potion to work."

The young woman nodded, tying everything up in a white piece of cloth and shoving it into her bra for safe keeping.

"How long will it take to work?"

"All great magic takes good time," replied the old woman with an enigmatic twinkle in her eyes. "Come back after this raining season, after you have harvested the crops which you planted in your fields and you can tell me whether this potion has worked or not."

And so it was to be.

Nattu and I gasped, barely able to contain our curiosity at how this tale would end. We, however, both remained silent.

"Ah... my little *fufu* heads are learning to hold their tongues and think first and then speak," Vatete continued. "There are two kinds of women – those who speak first, then think and regret their words. We call these children."

50

We burst out laughing because we knew ourselves as guilty of this.

"Then there are wise women who think a lot and speak very little. These are the kinds of women who find great success in life, in business and in love."

Vatete's piercing gaze could magically see right through me: "You have a question Chi?"

"Well yes Vatete... it's... mmmmh... it's about..." I blushed looking down.

"Sex," Nattu finished my sentence. "How can you write about these things, but be too shy to ask Vatete? In face I will read to you some of her thoughts."

Nattu laughed at my dismayed look.

The Emotion of Sex
10 Reasons Why He Is In Lust, But Not In Love With You

Image credit: FashionBank.ru

"I want you!" He moaned.

One of the biggest mysteries for women about men is that which surrounds their emotion of sex. The emotion of sex is tricky because it is the mistress to love, but mimics the real emotion. A man in lust is not in love with a woman. For strange reasons, women just refuse to understand this basic truth.

It would be far more prudent with self-preservation of our hearts in mind to learn more about this and raise our sexual IQ. So if you are frolicking along in a blissful relationship, don't be shocked if it's not about love, but sex for him.

Here are 10 Reasons 'Why He Is In Lust But Not In Love With You.'

#1 It's easier. The emotion of sex is easier than that of love for a man. Sex is straightforward. The premise is simple. Is she hot? Yes. Done deal. Love walks a more crooked road. Is she the one? This is a more complex question. The variables that must come together for a man to fall for you are more specific. It's easier to just shelf that one for a rainy day and just enjoy you for casual sex. So when he text messages you that he wants you, he is in lust and not in love with you.

#2 It's faster. The emotion of sex can come over a man in seconds. Love takes time. So the most practical thing is to assume that if things are still hot and new, he is operating off lust and not love. That is not to discount love in the future, but for the moment he is certainly more likely in lust and not in love with you.

#3 It's cheaper. The emotion of sex for a man is a cheaper investment than love. This is highly appealing. Not only can he have your body as if he were in love with you and you with him, but he can check out the instant the act is over. Love lingers like cheap perfume and, for right now, he would like for all of you to leave out at once. Obviously he is in lust and not in love with you.

#4 It's PC. The emotion of sex is politically correct and encouraged amongst men. Even women in their infinite foolishness have begun to validate this emotion as acceptable. The problem lies in pretending that it's love. It's not love honey; it's lust.

#5 It's fun! The emotion of sex is always accompanied by lots of excitement and fun. This is a positive reinforcement that validates lust. Love is usually accompanied by drama, fighting, jealousy and demands. It's sane to seek out pleasure and to avoid pain. So chances are that he is subscribing to lust and not to love with you.

#6 It's open! The emotion of sex is open and affords the guy a lot more freedom. In this state of mind, a man can comfortably pursue several playmates at once. The emotion of love is often closed minded and so the guy would be pretty much just tied to one partner. With that said, it makes sense why he picks to be in lust over being in love with you.

#7 It's a copy cat. The emotion of sex mimics love with all the perks and few of the downsides. It is sweet and charming. It can woo you with dinner dates and gifts. It feels great and can make you forget that love exists. It says complimentary things. It treats you perfectly. It texts and calls you. It makes you happy and smile to yourself. It's on your mind. It misses you. In fact, it has every aspect that love has, except it's not love. It's lust.

#8 It's popular. The emotion of sex is like the younger, sexier, more playful version of love. It appeals to men on so many levels that it's power and popularity is undeniable. So you might want to switch gears because you are headed for heartache if you are operating off different emotions. The odds are very high that he is just in lust and not in love with you.

#9 It's unconventional. The emotion of sex has a bigger playground. There are endless possibilities of how it can play out. In love it's cut and dry. Date. Get engaged. Get married. This is the traditional route. Or date. Date some more. Keep dating. Either way, there is not much wiggle room here. But in sex, who knows what happens next. So he picks to be in lust and not in love with you for these reasons too.

#10 It's unisex. If we can figure it out as women, it might not be such a bad deal after all. The most important reason is that keeping deep emotions at bay can be liberating and allows for adventure and exploration. Furthermore, why should dudes have all the fun while we pine away for love? Love takes her time and sometimes doesn't even show up at all. Lust is always on time and ready to have a good time. So perhaps instead of feeling hurt or disappointed, we could switch gears from love to lust. Be in lust and not in love with him!

The Love Potion continued...

"This is very good advice Chi!" Vatete was evidently proud of me. "Dear, will you fetch me some bread with this tea?"

Nattu and I scrambled to meet her gentle request.

"Sex is for the Gods and for the bees." Vatete laughed out loud.

"What do you mean?" We spoke as we often did in union.

"I mean that we will discuss that in a much more advanced part of your training. We are still in the Kindergarten of love, my darlings." Vatete's voice was firm. "But I will finish my story."

We both nodded in enthusiastic delight.

"Nattu tells me she wrote something on catching a man?" Vatete laughed. "Share this with me first and then perhaps I can convince you that it all comes down to the best love potion in the world."

Super Bowl Sunday Weekend!
10 Ways to Catch a Baller! Special Girls Fantasy
Football Weekend!

"Men catch the ball. Girls catch the baller!" She said excitedly!

Quit your moaning and groaning, no-one wants to hear about how you can't find a man or how badly the one you are lucky enough to have treats you! Not this week-end boo, its Super Bowl Sunday A.K.A Hot Girls Special Fantasy Football Week-end! If you are not at the Roqstars Boutique having Celeb Stylist Bobby hook up your hair and the Fierce Erika B do your make-up... or kicking it with SpoiltGirlsClub at the Make-up Bar in Beverly Hills getting your war paint on... or anywhere making yourself look fierce for tonight and this week-end, exception only for single mom's awesomely taking care of their precious lil' darlings, I have one word for you... Dusty!!!

You need to shake the cobwebs off and get ready for the sexiest weekend of the year. The weekend that all those gorgeous, strong, sexy, fit and manly man whom we always wonder about come out to play! This is a man's man – the kind of man who would rather hang out with the boys than hear you whining. The kind of man who is in the gym breaking a sweat when you are at home eating ice cream and feeling sorry for yourself and getting fat.

The kind of man who honors the Bro Code before the You Know What Code, is self-confident and assured and the kind of man who doesn't need to chase girls because they chase him. In short the kind of man we all want.

Like a rare fish, this kind of man is not near the surface of the water with the frogs and all the funny fish and the only reason he is out this weekend is because of his first love and it isn't you yet... it's Football! At least he has a passion.

This is just about the only weekend of the year that you don't have to look that hard. Sexy handsome dudes are going to be all over the place. Let them watch their team catch the ball while you catch them!

Here are 10 Ways to Catch a Baller This Super Bowl Week-end!

#1 Look hot! Please, I beseech you. The only thing that needs to look torn up is the player getting the wind knocked out of him on the football field this weekend and not you! It's going to take all you are working with to get him to peel his eyes away from the TV screen for even a second to glance your way.

When he does, you are going to be on point! Hair done! Nails done! Toes done! Face done! Done! Done! At the end of the game, the only thing getting a pounding again should only be reruns of that player on the football team and not you! Get his number and let him chase you. Or you'll just be 'that girl!'

#2 Shut up! There is no way in hell you are going to catch a baller running your mouth during the football game! Shut up! There is nothing you could say to him that will be of interest, good luck even if it's that you have twins on the way that minute! Look good, don't talk and relax! Football games are really long, so you have hours to silently work your charm!

#3 B you are not transparent! Move your donkey booty from the TV; you are not see through. Do not parade like a pathetic puppet up and down in front of the screen, blocking the view. This will only make you look bad and be very annoying. If he misses a major play because of you, it's a wrap! So kick back and relax. Sip your wine!

#4 Go out to any random party, to the nearest pub with the sports channel, he'll go to your ex's house who cares! Just go somewhere where men will be gathered, watching the game. It's kind of wicked, but easy to catch fish, all hanging out in a large school. Consider the football game the irresistible bait, the location the net and go fishing. You won't need just manicured hands!

#5 Take a friend as you'll probably be bored to death. Talk in low, whispering voice and don't worry. They'll throw you a bone of a great commercial to keep you entertained. No one said catching a baller was a walk in the park. He loves football. Get used to it. This is the other woman you'll never get rid of, so get to know her and she just might be a cool friend in future!

#6 Wherever you go, you will be greeted kindly if you go bearing a peace offering and gifts! Take some beer and snacks! Simple! This is the staple diet of a baller and will get you through the door with your cute friend in tow!

#7 Google the names of the teams playing. This is because you will not be completely ignorant, but who cares. I hate football!

#8 Smile! And cheer when he cheers! Over the next few hours, this will begin to build a warm comrade between the two of you! The look in his eyes will be better than that look of lust or even love sick puppy. It's the look of respect because he considers you cool enough to be one of, and hang with, the guys!

#9 Have your 1 Minute Elevator Pitch ready! This is the only time that he is actually going to give you and when he does go! You are now playing in the big leagues girl. No one has time to listen to extra shit. Keep it short, fast and lean! He will definitely come back at half time for more and maybe your number too!

#10 Have fun! Even spectators have fun, it's a football game! So lean back, relax, smile, and breathe deeply. Don't block the screen and shut the heck up and enjoy Super Bowl Sunday Weekend! Chappelle once said, 'If you want to make a man happy, shut up! Make him a sandwich and play with his balls!' So this weekend, if you want to catch a baller: 'Shut up! Make him a sandwich and let him play with his ball!'

The Love Potion continued...

"This one is very funny girls!" Vatete laughed. "I hope your readers have a sense of humor like me."

We shrugged it off. We had a love potion to attain and were little concerned with anything else.

"Well, the seasons came and went and in no time the young woman began to notice a great change."

Vatete had pulled a half knitted sweater from thin air and was knitting away.

"Was her husband in love with her again?" Nattu asked sipping at her red wine.

"Qeqeqeqeqe," Vatete looked disapprovingly at our half empty wine bottled and we nudged each other, giggling and choosing to ignore her. After all, we were big girls.

"Indeed he was. They no longer fought, at night he made passionate love to her and, in fact, he was in the habit of coming home earlier than usual now just to enjoy the tranquility of their home after a long hard day of work."

"That is unbelievable!" We chanted. "But how? So the love potion worked? But what was in the love potion Vatete and did you bring us some?"

"So many questions, but only two sets of little stubborn ears!" She rebuked sweetly.

"Please Vatete!" We begged.

"Of course the love potion worked. But we must follow the young woman back to the old woman in my story to have these questions answered because, believe it or not, she was just as startled and bemused as both of you are."

"OMG," said Nattu to me. "Look this blog post is trending!"

I glanced over to the computer screen.

Unleash Your Inner Tomboy!
10 Reason why it's Sexy Not To Be Fussy

CTM

"I Don't Mind Walking In the Rain!" She laughed

Even the most 'girlie-girl' has an inner tomboy! That's the sleeve-rolling, punch-throwing girl inside of you who is not afraid to get her nails dirty, doing some hard work. A girl without an inner tomboy is like a handicapped person because sometimes life calls on you to pull off your eye lashes, take the wig off, slip out of the six-inch heels and face it head on.

Here are 10 Reasons why it's Sexy Not To Be Fussy.

#1 When it comes to grace under fire, do it gratefully. There is nothing more devastatingly attractive. So they have told every dirty lie about you behind your back. So she came into your life pretending to be a friend in need and stole your man. So you lost your job and your car got repossessed.

This is not the time to bleed massacre tears. Find the very center of your soul. Go back to the darkest moment in your life. You survived that, you will survive this. Put away all your fancy ball gown dresses for another season. Pull out some old, faded blue jeans, pull your hair back into a bun and straighten your back. It's going to take a hell lot more than this to bring you down.

Brace yourself for agony, pain and smile. One day you will wake up and feel nothing. Congratulations! You are now stronger and officially a bad-ass!

#2 When it comes to reinventing yourself, do it boldly. So you used to wear cute little girlie pink skirts, socks and crisp white shirts? Charming! Chop off all your hair, grab some baggy pants and a gorgeous body-hugging tee, layer it with an old shirt and top it with a sexy leather jacket.

When you walk into the room, your ex or your own mother should not recognize you. Once you strongly grasp the concept of your own power for personal transformation, turn it inside. You now have the last tool you need to make all your dreams come true.

#3 When it comes to helping others, this is the drug for depression. Find a local church and find out about their outreach program. You don't have to be a Christian. Join the volunteers in their little purple bus on a sunny Saturday afternoon, going to a local battered ladies shelter.

When you see those women, large tormented eyes, huddled in corners, some with children and nothing else left in the word, but memories of violence, you will be humbled. So your problems are not that bad. Roll your sleeves up, grab a bucket with soap and water and start mopping the floors. When you leave, they will have a clean place to shelter and your soul will be cleansed.

#4 When it comes to chasing your dreams, no-one has time to deal with a sniffling school girl. Toughen up! Chances are no matter what path you are on, they are millions others on it as well. So you have to get a clue. Save your little girl antiques for your man, but for the professional arena your inner tomboy would be better suited. You can still be a woman, but your inner tomboy is not about to submit to BS or be taken advantage of, so let her handle the business side of things!

#5 When it comes to finding your Inner David, she can take down any Goliath. Whatever the obstacle that seems insurmountable and requires a miracle, unleash your sexy inner tomboy! She understands that in boxing you always keep your guard up and she in not above using her charm to knock an opponent out cold.

She knows all your haters and always has your back. She can size up a situation and people quickly and accurately because her survival depends on it. But don't get it twisted; her boxing gloves are pink with Swarovski crystals.

#6 When it comes to collecting experiences like Souvenirs, she has learned from every single mistake that you ever made. That is why she is hardened and that leaves your girlie girl side freed up to be light, fluffy and sweet. Your sexy inner tomboy will never hold a grudge, but she will never make the same mistake

63

twice. This bold woman knows how to lift herself from the ground, dust herself off and move forward towards her destiny.

#7 When it comes to the bedroom, the lady is a tramp! You stick to being sweet, coy and innocent on the street. Your inner sexy tomboy has your back in the bedroom.

#8 When it comes to dating your man, you are the love of his life, his little princess. She is his BFF. Your sexy inner tomboy is whom he jokes with, plays a little rough with, watches the football game with and kicks it with. It is important that you know when to let her have center stage for a great relationship.

#9 When it comes to getting into shape, your sexy inner tomboy is the one who is breaking a sweat to get your lil' booty back in shape. Let her do her thang and you'll be back to crawling into your size zero jeans in no time.

#10 When it comes to taking responsibility as a grown-up, it is your sexy inner tomboy who steps up. All little girls have to grow up into big girls one day. All big girls need to know how to grow into unleashing their sexy inner tomboy when the occasion calls for it.

The Love Potion continued...

"Boring!" I snapped back. "This is way too important a part of this story to worry about that Nattu.

"I take it you young ladies are ready for me to continue?" Vatete peered at us patiently over her rapidly clicking knitting needles.

"Yes!"

"Well, many seasons had come and gone and the young woman fearing that she was almost out of her love potion returned back to the old woman in the village of Maputi to ask her for more."

We huddled closer to Vatete.

"The young woman removed her sandals at the door of the little mud hut as a sign of respect and entered it."

"I have been looking forward to your return," said the old woman. "How did the love potion work for you?"

"It worked!" The young woman cried joyfully. "Everything is better! We laugh, we talk, we make love and we often spend a lot of time together."

"Indeed." Responded the old woman.

"So I am here to get more"

"You do not need anymore," said the old woman. "In fact, you never needed it in the first place."

"But my marriage was falling apart and now all is well!" Argued the young woman. "I did everything you asked me to!"

"How horrible!" Nattu screamed. "To get a love potion and then when it starts to work, you can't get a refill... I don't get it!"

Vatete laughed warmly giving her a warm hug.

"This is where the story really gets interesting, but before I tell you the rest, I would like to hear some more of your questions girls."

"How do you make someone fall in love with you Vatete?" I asked. "This is what my tribe of girlfriends and I think about this topic."

Only A Heart Is Worth Stealing
10 Quick Tips!

"What do you do?" He asked curiously. "Steal Hearts!" She replied sheepishly!

One of the first things we all learn is all is fair in love and in war. To ignore this axiom is a handicap. A heart is a precious thing. To ask for it is like walking into a jewelry store and asking them to hand you a diamond. Laughable at best. To beg for it is in vain. To demand it is fallacy, but to steal one is perfectly permissible.

Most people do not live a life of crime, but to accomplish this mission, you will need to polish up on your basic pick-pocketing and burglary skills. This task is not for the faint of heart and is best achieved solo.

First, you must set your sights on a heart worth possessing. Secondly, you must case the conditions under which it is locked up. Carefully figure out the tools you will need to get the job done and do a simulated mental test run. Now that you are ready to undertake the most sophisticated heist of all times here are 10 Quick Tips!

#1 Make sure the object of desire is available. Any bank robber would be certain that there was cash in the bank before holding anyone up. Similarly case the individual carefully and make sure they still have a heart to steal. Some people are so damaged their heart is missing. Others have already had it taken by another. Only you can decide on the love box worth your time at the high risk involved in being a thief.

#2 Case the dude. Is there a wall? How height? If it's a safe box, how resilient? Will you require nimble fingers to crack a code or a truck load of explosives? Are the lights on? Is anyone at home? Are there surveillance cameras? How many? Where? Is there a guard dog? Does it bite? You are going to have to use your brain. Every heart is tucked away and secured in a unique way there are no sweeping formulas. Asking the right questions will help you decipher if you are up to the job or not. Wanting it with everything in you will help you devise a plan!

#3 Gather your arsenal! Are you going to need patience? Humor? Heat? Or pig headed stubbornness to penetrate Alcatraz? Make sure you have what it takes. It is pointless going for someone who will require you to scale the wall of China if you are petrified of heights or deep sea dive if you can't swim.

#4 Write down your plan. You will need a pretty simple, but effective plan. What is it you want to achieve? Some examples might be: 'Make him notice me. Get on booty call list. Make him my man.' Whatever it is, make sure it's an isolated singular mission. Even if it's a combination of things, achieve them one at a time.

#5 Find an example of a situation as similar to yours as possible and do your homework. How did that robber set up for and execute that job? Even examples of others' failures may be used to your advantage and save you a lot of aggravation. You are almost ready to steal perhaps your first heart.

#6 The art of camouflage is crucial. The last thing you must give is an inkling of your intentions. There must be nothing betrayed in the flicker of your eyes or the slight trembling of hands that you are about to steal a heart. A casual easy-does-it-manner will be necessary. As with any great heists, patience will be your biggest virtue. Smile, whistle and keep walking. The best pick pockets are incognito.

#7 The moment of truth itself will be swift. Once you have broken into the safe deposit box containing the heart, you will have bare minutes to finish the job before alarms go off. Once you have a heart in your possession, relax. It will be weeks, months and sometimes years before he realizes that it's gone.

#8 Walk, don't run. Even with the euphoric rush of conquest surging through your veins, nothing on the outside must give you away. Remain cool. Act the same way you have always acted. Don't boast or tell anyone. Bid your time and remain fun.

#9 The first sign you will have of success is when you start to catch him giving you a quizzical look. Smile. Change the subject. After all what thief in her right mind would share that she is in possession of stolen property?

#10 Deny! Deny! Deny! Any charges brought against you. In fact, don't even share your rap sheet of previous similar crimes if any exist. Keep doing what you do. Sleep lightly with one eye open and watch him sneak into your love-shaped box and try to steal your heart in turn.

The Love Potion continued...

"Well my dear. Love is a rare and precious thing," said Vatete. "It is something to be given as a gift. One cannot beg for it, borrow it or steal it."

"Vatete is so right," I said. "I know this because if the guy does not like you well... Let me read this next blog and see what you both think."

He Speaks Dog Bitch!
10 Ways He Shows He Doesn't Love You
Without Saying A Word

He said nothing.

Words are weapons often used to hide how we truly feel. So we learn to read in-between the lines. Sometimes there is nothing to figure out, except that silence is disinterest, not a brooding deepness. All dog owners know every single thing communicated by their pet without words. Learn to read your man without words.

Here are 10 Simple Ways for Him to Show You That He Doesn't Love You Without a Word.

#1 When he never calls, you just text. He is not interested. The sound of your voice is not music to his ears. It's better to text you because you will hear from the tone in his voice that it was all BS and he isn't into you. The fantasy where you have a text wedding, invite guests by text, say vows by text and go home to text each other forever... scratch it. Talking is the first step to a real relationship.

#2 When he never calls you back. Girl, if you leave any more voice messages, he will hear the crazy in your voice. Remember, when he plays them at once, they will start out sweet, then worried, confused, frustrated, annoyed, angry, forgiving, insistent, begging and finally the rumblings of a lunatic who doesn't need a response. She can talk to herself! You have played out an entire relationship in your head and a scope of emotions in the most pathetic monologue this side of the Grand Canyon.

#3 When he doesn't ask you about yourself, he doesn't want to know. You can't talk about football, sex and him all the time. You might as well erase yourself from existence and give him a clone. He'd never know the difference.

#4 When he disappears at weekends, super bowl, his birthday, Valentine's Day, during the week, for weeks, no he is not an intergalactic traveler. His only superpower is twisting the truth.

#5 When he doesn't hold your hand in public or kiss you, yeah he is ashamed to be seen with you. He also wants to leave the coast clear in case something better catches his eye. Not someone, something! women are objects to him.

#6 When he ignores questions, yes, he heard you. He is too much of a gentleman to lie to your face.

#7 When you limp into the restaurant bleeding with knives in your back and he doesn't comment. You sit all through dinner and he doesn't even ask you if everything is ok... he really doesn't give a flying rat's ass.

#8 When you tell him you lost your job and he doesn't blink and then changes the subject....

#9 When you ignore him for days and he doesn't look for you and when you see him again it's like you never skipped a beat...

#10 When you catch him staring at the waitress. Yes, he does think she is prettier than you and wishes that he could take her home.

The Love Potion continued...

"The thing with love potions, my dear, is they only work where true love already exists." Vatete said

"So in this story, Vatete, was there already love between this man and this woman?" I asked

"Yes of course. In fact, share with me one more story on how you define true love and I will finally finish my story because it is growing very late and, after my long journey, I am ready for sleep."

Perfect Love from Imperfect People
Here are 10 Reasons Why

Just as with Adam and Eve, virtually all ancient myths referencing creation begin with the split of polarities from an original state of wholeness. In New Zealand they say that Maori separates Rangi and Papa. The Chinese God P'an-Ku separated copulation between Yin and Yang and in Greek mythology the God Zeus cut the souls of mankind in half.

It's ironic that we live in pursuit of perfection and its sandpaper effect on eroding all the jagged idiosyncrasies which make us unique. Absent of which we no longer fit our other half if and when they cross our paths again in this lifetime or another. I believe the desire to find love to be the unalienable right of every heart to find its other half. Perhaps the purpose of such a separation is to create the inciting incident that pronounces the embankment of the journey we call life.

We live in a world where there are more self-help books than stars in the heavens and, granted, we may aspire to be more enlightened, but in this blog, I dig dipper than our superficial flaws and differences. Let us consider the pillars upon which love rests. A friend of mine once said find one you have friendship, find two you have a lover, but find all pillars and you have found your soul mate.

#1 We live in a society where the word imperfection has a strongly negative connotation. It's dirty and everybody wants to wash it off with therapy, life coaching or prayer. Now I am not suggesting that anyone thoughtlessly consumes a degenerate life in celebration of their weaknesses, but I am saying that life happens and no one – except a liar – escapes unscathed. Scars are beautiful in the eyes of true love because they're a road map of where you've been, not where you are going. What appears broken when you examine one puzzle piece is perfect when you find the place it fits.

The capacity and depth to empathize with another human being, without judgement and to see the light and chase the shadows in them is the spirituality of love. This is the first pillar. You will need to be an advanced spiritual being to let someone else in. A lot of religious people are alone because religion is exclusive.

#2 There are things which words cannot frame. There are inexplicable ways in which one may feel for another that words only seem to defame. The silent potion of this resonation between souls is chemistry. It is the complex emotional and psychological interaction between two people.

The affinity is not without friction. Yin and Yang are by definition radically apart. It's logic as to emotion, thinking as to feeling, and pursing as to surrender. A match box needs a match stick to spark fire. So honor the coming together of two individual souls because it will probably be a little capricious. Attraction is a nucleus pillar.

#3 The third pillar is intimacy. Now intimacy is a strange bedfellow because everybody has their own definition of it. For those of us who have been accused of not possessing this affluent relationship trait, how is this for a suggestion? You were with the wrong person. When you are with the right person there is no separation, no lack. You just are. It's a continuous presence that never leaves you which has nothing to do with being physically present with each other. Intimacy is just that odd familiarity from the beginning which compounds over time. It's being comfortably uncomfortable with each other.

#4 Next comes passion. Passion is the expression of chemistry. Sex is apparently the most linear and rudimentary outlet for passion. You will want to find higher being expressions of your passion in a soul mate relationship. This is because a soul mate will only gravitate to your highest energy frequency. Be virtuous. Get to know each other. Engage in courtship. After all, it's a tale as old as time, so old world rules apply. Passion is the bones of a good work of architecture. Sex is the extravagant chandelier that you hang when all else is sound.

#5 Down in the trenches at ground level is the next pillar. Values. Values are the personal codes of conduct by which one navigates their life. Values are who you are to yourself in sickness and in health, for richer or for poorer, until you depart from this life. Society has a diseased formula of what everyone's values should be. True values run thicker than blood. They are genetic imprints of whom you are, where you are from, how you came to be.

Were your ancestors' pirates ravishing the seas, slave owners or freedom fighters? The answer to these questions will lie in what you are predisposed to gravitate towards. If you are an enlightened being, your core values will never change, but will evolve to the greatest good of the greatest number of dynamics.

Unfortunately for women, we have being disenfranchised of being practitioners of our true value system in relationships. Everybody has heard about sexual exploitation, but there is a far more sinister beast called *value exploitation*. This is when a woman is subjected to the value system of a spouse which might contradict her own.

I call it a 'rape of morals' because oftentimes in the beginning, a potential mate will mimic your values to attract you then practice something contrary afterwards. The good news is ex's *value detox*. It takes two years for the oxytocin of being with someone to completely get out of your system. That's how long it will take to just practice who you are again. So when a man meets a woman, it would behoove him to ask her how long the separation period from the past has being.

#6 The above mentioned would be the meat of things. Now let us take a closer look at the skeleton of it. Both will need to co-exist. Physical is an easy target because it has been scientifically proven that men pick with their eyes. Women are advised by Dr. Pat Allen to pick with their ears instead, unless you are a cougar. You will know from first sight to first touch if the physical is within your spectrum of do's. You can't force polar bodies and expect an organic synergy. Impossible.

#7 Emotional intelligence (EI) is the next endoskeleton of this soul mate equation. EI is a hilarious subject that is no laughing matter at all when you are at the center of this vortex. If an adult could not count in chronological order or tell an apple from an orange, there would be room for concern. But you can be emotionally retarded and get along without obvious road-bumps until too comes to love.

In love it's so abstract it's like being required to speak an arcane language fluently which you never studied in school. Here are two people who do not have a uniform expression or love language attempting to at once reconcile themselves to all the complexities occurring and at the same time communicate them to another person; difficult at best.

It's easy to mislabel the other person's thoughts, reasons, and actions. It is even easier to send the wrong signals. This is because we all have our own internal guide of what certain things mean. Simple absence could wrongly spell rejection to one, while explicit enthusiasm might mark you certifiably insane to someone more reserved. This is when the intelligence quota kicks in.

It's important to remember why you are in a world of hurt. It's not for hate or war, it's in an attempt to bridge a love affair from stranger to more. Here is when it's crucial to laugh things off. This is the best time to view life as just a good old-fashioned comedy. After all, it's fun to learn a brand new language.

#8 A lack of a truly grounded intellectual connection is the first sign of a disconnected attachment. This is an area in which people often feel very comfortable to settle compensating themselves by drawing this energy from friends and work instead. It is not highly advised for one to pick a brainless co-pilot to fly at withering heights. How can one be surprised when they crash and burn? An intellectual bond is the playground of the imagination. This is where you can both go and play, dream and grow. This is the return to the lost Eden. The only serpent to be found here is boredom if you are not both equally engaged.

#9 At this point you strictly have everything which you need to discern if you have a soul mate connection. Unlike in the movies when all things are aligned it will be so powerful that it will equally attract and repel simultaneously. It's as if both halves feared to lose themselves in the whole. We are cultivated to transcend our own borders and to overcome challenges to have the honor to meet our soul mate. Yet when it happens fear will subconsciously or otherwise kick in.

This is the imperfect reaction which is ironically the best one. There is something to be feared. Marianne Williamson once said, "Our deepest fear is not that we are inadequate. Our deepest fear is that we are powerful beyond measure. It is our light, not our darkness that most frightens us. We ask ourselves, who am I to be brilliant, gorgeous, talented, and fabulous?" Such is the epiphany of love.

#10 Love is a colossal thing. It's certainly not for the faint of heart. I think that it's sad that most of us spend a lifetime just trying to grasp this part. So we spend a lifetime in the kindergarten of our love affairs. We look at this vehicle and the next never making a firm choice, and then we die.

We leave this life never having taken the journey with a soul mate. I believe that even marriage is a parked vehicle. People get married and that is the destination. Only when all things are aligned, will you be able to have the blazing cognition that finding a true soul mate is the beginning of a great adventure. All these pillars have little to do with just establishing a connection and everything to do with prescribing where that connection will take you. Children, pets, family and friends can come along for the ride, but they are not the end of all of it. So as I look around in the junkyard of parked relationships, I am not surprised that people are unhappy, unfulfilled and that things often end in goodbye. We operate at such a pedestrian level when it comes to love.

The Love Potion continued...

"Very good girls I am very proud of you," Vatete smiled lovingly. "So finally in grand conclusion to my story..."

"What do you mean? I cannot get a refill on my love potion? Whatever shall I do!" The young woman cried.

The old woman hobbled out of the mud hut and returned holding a bag of salt in one hand and another green pebble in the other.

"What is in this bag?" she asked

"Any fool can see that it is salt!" Snapped back the irritable young woman.

"Perhaps some fools, but not all, because this is what I gave you to sprinkle." The old woman laughed, revealing her toothless pink gums.

"And what it this?" She asked, holding out the green river pebble.

"Well that looks like a green river pebble, but this one has magic on it, right?"

"It appears to be a green river pebble because it is. The only magic that it ever had is the magic that you yourself ascribed to it and not I."

"But I don't understand..."

"Do you remember my instructions?"

"Yes but..."

"So for many seasons you have been rising up at the crack of dawn to bath and late at night so your hygiene is impeccable. You have been cleaning around the house and outside your hut twice a day and you have been preparing your man a hearty meal"

A look of understanding began to enter the young woman's eyes.

"Ahhh..."

"And above all, every time you think of harsh words you remain silent until the anger washes over you and you can speak to your young man with a sweet tongue again."

Nattu and I giggled delightfully at the unexpected ending to the story of the secret magic love potion.

"So the magic has been in your actions and the love potion in your changed behavior." The old woman sniffed her tobacco. "Now if I had said to you, you must get up early and clean your home and hold your tongue, you would not have listened to me because you wanted a quick fix."

The woman nodded bowing her head down in humble acknowledgement of this sage woman.

"So I gave your common table salt and a common pebble to give you the desire to adjust your behavior and, after all these seasons, these are now good habits which you have formed are they not?"

The young woman laughed.

"So please go away from my hut and remember that the love potion is in being loving and lovable to that you might be loved in turn."

Vatete closed her eyes softly drifting off to sleep.

"Wow," Nattu spoke softly. "I am so excited to hear what she will teach us tomorrow."

"She is absolutely magnificent." I agreed turning the lights off.

Unlocking Your Hidden Potential!
10 quick tips on how to manifest your true love and destiny!

CTM

"I love you!" she whispered.

Love is a journey that begins with self-love and ends very far from where it started. Fairy tales, romantic comedies, romance novels and many silly little girls seem to think that love is stuck on the "*me*" button. Unlock your true potential; find your true love and destiny in 10 simple steps! But first all the things they never told you about what love really is.

#1 "I wish you loved me!" She thought. This is the very first kind of love. It is characterized by selfishness and all expression is internalized. "Me, me, me!" love is also a form of emotional masturbation. The nucleus of this kind of love is the ego.

#2 "I Love You!" She said. This is the second kind of love. It is characterized by mutual gratification. I'll give if you take and give me back love. At core it is still narcissistic in true form. "You, me, you, me!" love is a mirror love. The other person is nothing more than a pseudo partner and an emotional boomerang to bounce back love and energy. All you'll ever look for and see in a mirror is yourself. Not the other person. This is an external expression of self serving love.

#3 "I don't love you!" He said; external expression of self preservation. A lesson in separation and in letting go! Selfless. "You, you, you!" Self neglecting and not giving but not taking either. Positive in the sense that for the first time the mirror love is shattered. Seeing two separate people not self. The realization that love feels good and is wanted but not needed for survival. New kind of love encountered... love of freedom and independence from partner.

#4 'I miss you!" She said. Internal expression of love. A desire for reconciliation is the pre action mechanism produced by a manifestation of restless inner emotion. At this stage in the love journey one explores individuality. Love for partner is unconditional and unprovoked. This love gives before it takes. Lessons in appreciation of partner as a separate entity, not an extension of emotional self catering to the "*me*" love and understanding of love as a true gift, not a right.

#5 "I love them!" She thought. This is the 5th step in the love journey and may be expressed both internally and externally. This kind of love focuses entirely on community building. This love is of genuine service to others and focuses on the greatest good to the greatest number of dynamics. The individual engaged in this process feels accomplished and fulfilled.

In this stage of love you discover your talents, life purpose and destiny. So many women spend all their time crying over men and waiting for "the one" who in actuality is nothing more that the image of their selfish desires reflected in their mirror of choice! It's not unlike retesting and repeating first grade all your life and not even knowing there is an amazing life and career after school!

#6 "I feel connected to all love!' she said. Divine love is internal and reflected as external and as omnipresent too. One may feel as if they were an instrument of a higher calling. Humility is the virtue acquired at this juncture in the love road. Geniuses exist in this state of being. This is the state in which innovative ideas are channelled through an individual. The vessel, as it were, does not need to feel ownership or even as the source of original genius concepts.

One in this coveted place merely views self as a custodian entrusted with valuable knowledge from the all knowing universe. Selflessness in this state is essential so as not to limit the "*spark of genius!*" to merely what is contained by the recipient. In the karma cycle one gets back hundredth fold all the good which one has put out.

Monks often fast for days to simulate this enviable state of consciousness. This state may only be attained in the awesome power of now! Jesus is an example of someone who clearly displayed stage 6 love.

#7 From stage 6 most people often come back full circle to their core, the "I'. This time around "I love you!" is a higher expression. An example of this kind of love is what a woman might feel for an ex husband. In this circulation love seeks to inspire and not to marry!

Ironically in denying selfish pleasure a more acute feeling of love is experienced. This love is 100% selfless. Unconditional wants nothing in return. In not needing love to be reciprocated, love wants to and is indeed reciprocated.

#8 "I love to make..." she said. This is the truest form of love! The purest and highest level of self expression is the level of creation. In this place we have an opportunity to make mortal emotions immortal by expressing them in their most selfless form. All an artist does in voice, painting or in poem is to *give, bleed and give, and then give and give some more*! In this state we emulate our creator and, in doing so, we find our ultimate destiny.

In this place we feel internally and in equal proportions to this emotion we manifest externally. In our intellectual context we create and in our biological sub context we procreate. Our sexual energy is our mystical metaphysical energy expressed as its lowest common denomination!

Mozart, Di Vinci, Picasso, Shakespeare, Socrates and Andrea Brochelli are a few examples of exceptional individuals who achieved this extremely high level of ingenuous love!

You will require a mastery of all previous 7 stages of love to create your own comprehensive masterpieces! Creation is the combination of all previous influences of love, acting on the creator, in varying degrees.

Bad art is created at stage 2 the "*me, me, me, me, me!*" It fails to impress in that it does not transcend the "*me!*" to encompass the entire human experience therefore we cannot relate. Iconic and great art is effortlessly created at stage 8. Its pricelessness lies in the artists' ability to make it all about the rest of us for till the end of time.

#9 "I destroy!" she said angrily. This route takes one back to the childhood state of daydreaming or *creation in procrastination*. The opposite and more positive side of this would be back to the beginning of the journey "I wish you loved me!" Destruction in this sense is not necessarily a bad thing. It is merely an agent of change that resets the clock back to start. You will keep recycling through this process until you find your inner light aka your God given "gift".

The lower level fear expressed manifestation of this higher calling is looking for "the one" What you are really searching for is your God given "gift" not a man to make you whole. Desire for a man is the illusion created by the mirror effect. A lot of women force themselves to stay stuck at this rudimentary stage all their lives. In this place creativity is condensed into a more animalistic sexual energy.

Procreation is an acceptable substitute for creation. The masterpiece of a brand new human life is our higher self nudging and reminding us to not give up but to continue on our journey to our higher calling. A baby is the external symbolization of our God given hidden inner "gift." Interestingly, children can often continue the forfeited journey their parents began. In instances they are the ones rewarded with the amazing "gift!"

We all have a gift but we do not all have the courage to continue on our journey until we reach our goals. For once energy is created it cannot be destroyed. Although we do have freewill, the authentic purpose of the universe carries on its prescribed course uninterrupted with or without us.

#10 "I keep creating!" ad infinitum! This is the most perfect expression of love and uninterrupted equilibrium! *"God"* would be an example of a being that exists in this perpetual state of alpha and omega. This grand expression of love is *"the eternity!"* The mind bedazzling reality of a universe contained within a universe and so forth. With our finite minds it is hard to imagine something without an end. Yet it must be so because whatever galaxies we know are contained within others.

There's no sudden stop in the form of a brick wall because even that would need to take up a space outside of its own perimeters to exist. Mind boggling! Perhaps that's why it's easier for us to wallow in simple matters of the heart like the old age classical cliché tradition of *"He loves me and he loves me not!"* :) xo

Yin Man and Yang Woman

CTM

"Tell Me What You Think!" He yelled.

"I Feel That You Might Be Upset," she responded.

The dichotomy between men and women is a tale as old as time. As a general cliché, men think about how they feel and women feel about how they think. With this said it is a potential land mine of miscommunication waiting to happen. It is therefore important to be diligent and self aware of each other as different but equal and unequal to equal proportions to truly understand the opposite sex in the context of love, sex, dating and long term relationships.

The first myth that I must debunk is the one that men are men and women are just women. We now live in a world where often times women are men in beautiful bodies and men are gentle females trapped inside a rough exterior. And I am not making reference to sex changes or the Gender challenged but about the varying degrees of masculine and feminine energy that makes up every man and woman on the planet.

A single mom forced to survive the harsh climate of the economic world as a bread winner will need to cultivate more aggressive "male based" traits like ambition and a ruthless go-getter attitude whilst an artist type dude living off his wealthy family might exude a more gentle homemaking aesthetics about himself. Yin is the term which denotes the female energy in us and Yang is attributed to the masculine side.

Here are ways to know if you are a Yin man or a Yang woman in romance.

#1. To test my theory, simply ask yourself if you often feel more "like a Tomboy?" (Yang Woman) or a "girlie guy?" (Yin Man). Be brutally since honest this is only between you, yourself and this book.

#2. In your dating dance do you often find yourself impatient for the guy to make the first move and taking more of an initiative in asking a hot man out on a date? Then you are a Yang woman.

#3. You are a strong busy guy but when you get home you love to pou"I spy with my little eyes something beginning with L!" She Said.

I spy with my little eye something beginning with R! While we may not all have a degree in Criminology or Law, we are all blessed with instinct.

If you suspect your man is chasing after someone else's cheese, here are 10 things every LPI (Lady Private Investigator) should know on how to catch that rat!

#1 The Trash Can Never Lies! So you have cursed the house, waited for him to go to work, called his office and confirmed he is in meetings all day. You have switched out your natural locks for a blonde white girl wig, blue contacts and a house keepers outfit. You are ready to scale the wall, disarm the alarm and enter his crib. Your pink Tom Tom's make your Indian name floating feather. Without further ado, dive deep into his trash can.

"Mmmmmmmh something is a-foot!" Yes tampon wraps, make up removers, and yuckie used condoms might indeed be a red flag if you, like cat-woman, have made it this far. Unfortunately, us mere mortals will have to stick to casing the man. To get to know a man, dig up the trash can of his mouth in anger. Most women make the mistake of screaming to make their point when they should be listening to his!

What names does he call you? What did his ex do that you do? Why he is never home on time and what is the problem with your weight again. And there you have it. You are being compared to someone he still loves, is in love with or will love in the future. Pack it up. It is only a matter of time now, and a lady never overstays her welcome.

#2 A Closet Never Lies! Now the closet search is not for the faint hearted! If she lives there, or frequents him often, you will find her red bottoms and Hugo Boss here! Oh yeah bitches like this always have the shit you pray for and wish he would get or you....well he can't he is getting it for her! Time for some tough love. Check the drawers as well. No, those are not his clothes that shrank in the washing machine. He has kids! And the hardest thing to find in the closet is your man! Sorry, boo.

#3 A Medicine Cabinet Never Lies! So how long has your man been on birth control? Wow!

#4 A Car Dashboard Never Lies! If that is his favorite juicy couture scent or lipstick color, girl you are in trouble! He has bigger secrets to share with you. You thought he was cheating on you with some girl, but he is the other woman! Run! Next!

#5 A Cell Phone Never Lies! A man's phone is dangerous. You cannot come back from what you will find here. This is no man's land, because what you find here you cannot un-see. Text messages and missed and made call logs are all damning evidence. I once knew an especially bright guy... he tried to convince me that I had read the message wrong.
 But a smart girl sends all texts to herself to brood over with the pack later. Some flowers and a lot more clever lie later; the truth is that the trust is already lost. This is a two way street. You violated his privacy. He violated your heart. A match made in hell?

#6 A Wallet Never Lies! From credit cards you didn't know he had, to business cards from other women, to all the damning dinner for two receipts when he was having Boys Night Out. Gosh He Must Love that boy! That sensation you are feeling is called falling out of love. It is that heart sinking, bile rising in your throat, heart beat slowing down for dead, deep in your belly it is over feeling. The last four steps are just to nail his coffin shut...no-one likes an ex coming back from the dead! They stink!

#7 A Pocket Never Lies! Much like a wallet, a man's pockets always tell on him! Match sticks from some hotel resort, a number scribbled on a paper in pretty writing, and for the real dada heads keys to Motel 6!

#8 A Facebook Status Never Lies! So he wants it to say single. Why? His boss should not care dime! Or those comments from Lucy and Becky... no woman is just liking a man for kicks, honey doll. And that "Friend" clinging to him like a drowning man at every major event is not his favorite sister Becky! And the real pigs that block their timelines so no-one can leave messages please go and sit down! The other woman's time line is loaded with your photo's and screen shots of all your texts. smh. Where can a good cheater run and hide these days? Inbox me for $100 to winner!

#9 Match.com Never Lies! Baby Doll, his mama did not have two of his ugly ass! That is not his evil uglier twin! Yes it's his big Gucci denying head on Match! His profile reads like...the BS he told you on your first date! He suddenly has a higher income bracket and his unemployable ass is CEO of what? Lies Inc? Ok. So those are lovely pictures taken a few years ago when he was on roids and had a little hair. And that is not a bad look in his friend's boat taken on the Lake.

Mmmmmh that suit you got him for his birthday is his best look. He is still 49? And he wants a woman with a college degree and is intelligent but won't however have the mind to catch him at his lies! He last spoke to his mom last Thanksgiving but he is a family man and in his dreams, he loves to race cars for fun. For kicks, create a profile too and respond to him re-introducing yourself and see if the asshole will fall for you twice!

91

#10 The Heart Never Lies! By the time that you went searching for my book, you already knew. There is no lens that can see deeper than the heart. Yes, you are over 30. Yes, you thought, perhaps. Of course dating is a chore. And it is going to hurt like a rat's ass. What can I say? At least you have the skills to open a very successful Private Investigation firm!

All your girlfriends are popping out babies at the speed of light but you just want a career. You might consider kids later but the thought of dirty diapers makes yours skin crawl? Yang Woman.

It is a silly romantic movie that your girlfriend made you watch (as well as all those Sex in the City Reruns you indulge her with paying attention to) and when the season ended well you would never let her see but you felt yourself kind of tearing up... Yin Man.

If you have to pick between a boxing match with the boys or secretly watch the winter figure skating with the bedazzled outfits, you would rather pick the later.... Yin Man. When you were growing up you were raised to do good above feeling good and now even though you have a cool boyfriend you'd rather call the shots than follow his lead... Yang Woman.

You are going to be late getting off work so you step outside and call your girl telling her that you feel sad that you won't be home in time for dinner Yin Male.

Your boyfriend is working on a business deal and he mentions it to you to get your feedback and asks you what you think so you proceed to with ruthless precision tell him that it is a really crappy stupid idea and why... Yang Woman.

You are madly in love and you can't wait to spend your lives together but only under one condition. He will stay at home and raise the baby. Yang Woman.

You just adore your Granny and listening to all her good old stories. In fact you speak to her as many times a day as she calls you but you a big burly bearded guy. Yin Man.

There is no right or wrong to what we are but a great relationship exists on a see saw balance. Even in gay and lesbian relationships one partner must take on the "male" role while the other must be more "feminine" to avoid butting heads. So in love if you are a man trapped inside the body of a beautiful woman dating a sweet girl who is in a tough guy body who cares! Just understand who leads and who follows who down the aisle.

Kick His Ass To The Curb!
10 Reasons Why Rebound Dogs Have Rabies!

We are all the by-products of circumstances and the villains or victims of time. In love especially we have taken far too much credit of the outcome and not enough responsibility in the instances of war. Of far less importance in the successful acquisition of true love is our beauty, our charm or our obsessive desire to possess it.

Instead, it is an elusive moment in time which is often the appointed captain of our destiny. It is some forgettable happenings in the past that prescribe the course of our actions in the future. Indeed it is only in the many broken pieces of our hearts that we may finally hope to find an unlikely masterpiece.

Although it is certain that in making most of our mistakes today, the next day is blessed merely by virtue of its random placement in the future. In hind sight the miracle of clear vision comes to the blindness which is the nature of love. Thus a man is rewarded with fortune less by merit to self but more by the fated place in the circle of life he finds himself when the opportunity to love is suddenly bestowed upon him. Beware then of the slight and passing moment before the perfect moment. Kick his ass to the curb no matter how sexy, successful and gorgeous he is!

10 Reasons why rebound dogs have rabies!

#1 A rabid dog looks very angry and drools at the mouth! You will know he is mortally wounded by the scowl on his face. His lips will be knitted into a snare rather than surrender to a simple smile and this will be on the first few dates. What eats him ate him and has nothing to do with you. However he will still bite even though unprovoked. You could be mother Theresa with double D's and it will mean nothing. He is rebounding from a nasty break up and you are for sure about to catch a slap meant for a bitch!

#2 Stay well aware you will get bitten! Women love to approach wounded animals. There is a maternal instinct to heal, but ignore it! The sexual tension and excitement will soon be replaced by pain. Yours. He might formulate his romantic pursuit of you around an imaginary love but alas the truth will soon be revealed. The initial subconscious rebound reflex which will manifest itself in your lover to be will be mighty offensive! Duck and let this jiggered boomerang complete its karmic course. The sacred in him will seek to be avenged and your bleeding heart will make an acceptable sacrifice. Walk away.

#3 If affronted by his rebound rabid self whilst minding your own business you will have no choice, but to hit him with hard words and chase him away. Be firm. Your happiness is on the line. Tell him that he is rebounding and therefore diseased and you have no interest in partaking in his misery. Do not succumb to a tender feeling of weakness nor let a flicker of sympathy show across your face. This will be his cue to pounce and he is going for your jugular!

#4 Rebound rabies from the Latin word "madness" is the dis-ease a man feels when the afflictions of his broken heart spread to his brain. Unfortunately, the emotional virus can be spread from man to woman without difficulty if the woman comes into immediate contact with the tormented victim soon after the ending of a previous relationship.

In no time heartache, fighting headaches, acute pain, violent actions and depression appear.

Roughly 97 percent of all rebound rabies in women occurs because ignoring all the obvious signs they have entered into a love relationship with a calloused and cheeky rebounding man.

Again it's not your fault but you are nothing more than a temporary punching bag. It is the next relationship after you in which he will be healed and normal.

#5 The symptoms expand to slight or partial paralysis, anxiety, insomnia, confusion, agitation, abnormal behavior, paranoia, terror, hallucinations, progressing to delirium.

#6 Dormant rabies can be found in a rebound guy. This is probably the most dangerous! This is the "I'm fine!" guy. The smiling "I don't care" guy who really is delusional enough to think that he is not affected.

A simple diagnosis can be made by you to check if this is true. Watch closely to see if there are unexpected bursts of anger, erratic mood swings from cool to bummed or the classical vacant "no-one home" staring at the wall. Run!

#7 If you suspect that you might be even remotely infected by osmosis, immediately go to your most positive girl friend and shake it off. (Emo – osmosis here defined as the diffusion of emotions through a semi permeable membrane from rock bottom depression to an emotional state with a higher energy frequency until there is an equal concentration of feelings of sadness and hopelessness on both sides.)

As you already know, misery loves company.

#8 Prevention, of course, is the best cure. Stay away. Immunize yourself by raising your guide and thinking of the last asshole you dated. Show no love this is not your problem! You refuse to pay for another woman's crimes in your spare time.

#9 For further prevention, you might also consider vaccinating the rebound guy! Lots of casual meaningless sex if you go in with your wits about you and nowhere near emotional is the best vaccination for him.

Just remember that you will be doing this for the next girl. A mercy act.

#10 Not handling stray men whose backgrounds you do not know is a really good prevention policy. if it is someone you know simply contact his previous handler and get the break up scoop to determine what you are dealing with.

     In dating you can keep a close eye on the local dating scene to make sure you stay clear of the rabid rebound guy.

Marriage is the act of getting your man neutered in the most permanent and severe method of rabies prevention. Men that are sterile are less likely to leave home, become strays, and reproduce more stray rabid rebound men.

Why You Can't Find 'The One' Because It's An Imaginary Lover 10 Great Reasons

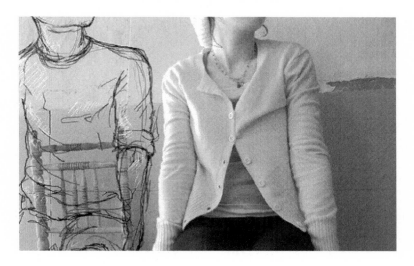

"I think he is 'the one!'" she gushed.

Long after the friend who always ate your greens at the dinner table has vanished into thin air. Eons after the man in the sky with a long white beard is done dishing out miracles and the chubbier one supposedly fond of chimneys is hit hard by the recession and stops bringing gifts ...

Past the token giving tooth fairy, the chocolate hiding Easter bunny and the generous three wishes granting genie retires lingers one die-hard imaginary friend..."the one!"

The One inspires awe and excitement by the mere mention of his name and he rarely if ever has to earn his privileges they are just bestowed upon him. The One is much more dashing than simple Prince Charming who of course is always late to an engagement even one as important as rescuing a damsel in distress. The One is infallible. The One is even a notch above the God who created him and perhaps therein lies the seeds to his eminent downfall. Even as we grow up and leave behind the scarred veteran bears of our childhood, One Eye McPee, Honey No Legs Bunny and Whitney no heart McFluffy... few of us ever outgrow our closest childhood imaginary friend...the enchanting guy of our dreams. So is it a wonder you keep longing and waiting for him to turn up in vain?

10 Great Reasons Why You Can't Find 'The One' Because It's An imaginary Lover!

#1 Like all of your imaginary friends, he is a childhood construct. He is the carefree youthful spirit from a time before you knew about bills and good and bad guys were categorized simply into cowboys and Indians!

#2 Like all of your imaginary friends, no-one else can see him but you. In your mind's eye he is as tangible and real as the day is long and he knows all of your secret musings and is swift to satisfy your every need. You've spend hot summer days laying out eyes closed delighted by just the thought of him.

#3 Like most imaginary friends, he has outlived his socially acceptable period of existence. Yes he was very acceptable when you were a teenage girl but now you hide him like a sordid sin from the concerned enquiries of friends and family.

#4 Although invisible, 'the one' is not an easy presence to dismiss. He is the unseen measuring stick by which you evaluate everyone you meet and try as your suitors might none come even close to the awesomeness and soul mate material quality of your imaginary lover.

#5 Although deterring you from giving more regular guys a fair chance with you in the real world, he himself is not subject to any laws of the universe. He is not confined by space, restricted by distance nor impressed upon by the hardships of the times. Instead he lives effortlessly immortalized by your sheer will power.

#6 Look closely at this old and trusted companion for, alas, he could indeed be an unknown foe. His lingering presence haunts you making it very difficult for you to come to grips with the now and impossible to see when some-one good is in front of you.

#7 As with all imaginary friends, his existence is solely based on your co-dependency to what he represents. This addiction expecting perfection from men you date always leaves you searching for something elusive and never content. As harmless as you might have thought it was to nurture this childhood nostalgia of a man...it could single-handedly be what is wrong with your love life.

#8 Oftentimes girlfriends will validate the existence of 'the one' by questioning you as to whether or not you think we have found him manifested in the flesh yet. In contrast men will often roll their eyes and refer to "the one' tongue in cheek. Either way he must be exorcised before you can hope to replace him with a real man.

#9 It is sad to let go of most things especially a close friend who has been as perfect as 'the one'! There

101

will be no fighting on his part, or name calling but a gallantly silent exit from your life when it is time. Trust indeed in this instance that when one imaginary man exists a real man enters the picture.

#10 I guess with childish naivety it is easy to miss the fact that you cannot look for something you already have. The healthy use of your imaginary lover is to help you formulate a working blueprint in your emotional minds-eye of the qualities that you look for in a male counterpart. Period.

To have babies and built a white picket fence with this hologram is insane. It is only a flawed, ass scratching and often times under sensitive man with feet of clay who can ever come close to making your dreams a reality. So the sooner you put away the most wanted poster of "the one" in your dreams, the sooner you'll stop scaring off the guy of your blissful waking moments.

10 Commandments of Dating

"Thou Shalt Have No Other Bitches & Whores Before Me!" She insisted.

So summer is almost over in the blink of an eye and you have committed all the 7 Deadly Sins...several times over. You are no-where nearer finding truelove by the next winter. If, however, this summer you were diligent in avoiding the 7 Deadly Sins then you are more than worthy of knowing the 10 Commandments of Dating This Coming Fall!

These rules are applicable to him and it is his discipline in observing them that will determine the longevity of your relationship. If indeed he has avoided the 7 Deadly Sins and he is not addicted to them it will be a whole lot easier. If he has not then he has cheated both himself and you because following the 10 Commandments of Dating will be impossible.

#1 Thou shalt have no other bitches and whores before your girl! Of course the only place we can start is with the most important dating command. No Bitches and Whore before girlfriends! What woman could possible not make this, not so simple to follow it seems, request! By definition the dating relationship does not even commence until this is established.

#2 Thou shalt not call me a bitch in vain! As far as name calling goes both people in the relationship have to work hard at not over indulging. It's a bad habit and a hard one to shake but call a bitch a bitch enough times...and she'll be a bitch!

#3 Thou shalt remember to keep date night fun and unholy! Realistically speaking if you both cannot make time for date night once a week...how are you dating?! The inability to commit to spending time and getting to know each other is an obvious red flag. However, it is your responsibility as the one who has been desperately looking for love in all the wrong places to make sure that this night is crazy FUN! Use your imagination, creativity and resourcefulness to impress your guy. Don't fool yourself this is an audition.

#4 Thou shalt honor thy mother. If your guy talks poorly about his mother be observant. Yes not all women make great moms. Yes he might have had a terrible childhood. Granted he does not have to like or even love her. However, when all is said and done a man whose bottom line is not honor for the woman, no matter what a monstrosity she was, who gave life to him is not a real

104

man. Honor is above respect because it cannot be earned respect can. Honor is by virtue of the giver not the given. Honor is his gift of respect to womanhood. It is indicative of how he will honor you. Especially when you make mistakes, lose your figure bearing his children and it all hangs loose with the gravity of old age.

#5 Thou shalt not kill! To kill is to deprive of life. Never take away the essence of what makes your partner tick, this is paramount to murder. In many ways expecting someone to change is a form of murder. Change is what we do for others. Grow is what we do for ourselves.

#6 Thou shalt not commit adultery. Adultery is the act of sex between two consenting adults one of who is lawful attached to another person. Adult implies a grown up act when in reality it is one the most childish mistakes to make. Of course what makes us adults is realizing that our actions have consequences. So ponder what havoc this might wreak to your dating life.

#7 Thou shalt not steal a heart thou doesn't want. All is fair in love and war except when love is really war! Stealing the affections of someone you are not interested in is beneath a common criminal. At least they want what they steal.

#8 Thou shalt not lie. If you cannot be honest with each other in a relationship forget about it. It's just a matter of time before it's over and what a royal waste of time.

#9 Thou shalt not covet thy neighbor's partner. The moment you let one deadly sin in...open the door roll out the red carpet the other 6 are in tow! What good could come from thinking that someone else's partner is better than yours?! If you drive away your own happiness then you are a lost cause.

#10 Thou shalt not covet thy neighbor's bent. Now there is a recipe for depression during these hard times wishing that you had more materially. If love and not the blue bus is not good enough to bring you home...then your entire life is meaningless.

Love Is Not A Charity!
10 Things He Will Do When Is He Too
Cheap To Date

"I forgot my wallet at home!" He lied.

Let me just cut to the chase broke ass dudes I am not talking about you. Yes, a girl can love a poor man who knows one day the fates might smile on him. I am NOT talking about being broke, poor or jobless. I am talking about *cheap*. By my definition cheap is some-one who *has* the ability to do something for you but would rather not. There! I have shade light on this topic so hold off on the hate mail my mailbox is full. Every woman deserves a man who adores her with all of his might, love and pockets!

#1 He is too cheap to date when he asks you out to an expensive place, orders lobster then claims that he left his wallet at home! Say "No problem Sweets! I gotchya!" Stand up and bounce gracefully out of the place without a backward glance.

#2 He is too cheap to date when he gives you something that belonged to some-one else for your birthday, V-day, Christmas or whatever. How will you know? When it is not in your style and remind you of his EX...too outrageous? Don't fool yourself, Hell Yes He Would! Bounce!

#3 He is too cheap to date when his imagination is broke! Not everything is a Louis Vuitton bag or a Benz you fool! Have you ever heard of picking wild flowers?, a picnic basket or a poem? Well If not then *next* in line might have a bigger brain forget the wallet. Bounce!

#4 He is too cheap to date when he tells you you don't look good with your own hair but he doesn't offer to buy you a weave! He should be kissing your big booty for been so low cost! Bounce!

#5 He is too cheap to date when he tells you that he doesn't like how you dress but he won't take you shopping. A man who makes you feel ,in his presence, like other women are the shit whilst your dusty ass trails after him at a party deserves to burn in hell! Bounce boo!

#6 He is too cheap to date when he buys himself a drink when you are with him and then acts like he doesn't like women who drink too much. Stop sipping on iced water trying to pretend, he *is* laughing at you inside. Bounce! Let him chase women who drink champs to maybe say Hello!

#7 He is too cheap to date when he gives you exact change when he asks you to go and buy him something. Seriously? Even runners get paid.

#8 He is too cheap to date when he starts a fight just before dinner time. Obviously you are both too upset to eat and then he acts like nothing happened but dinner really didn't happen and you spend the night hungry. That growling sound is your stomach begging you to bounce.

#9 He is too cheap to date when he can't even be generous with his bloody words. So you have a third eye, two horns and you occasionally breath fire? Who cares?! Not him when you are laid up in his bed. Bounce Girl Bounce!

#10 He is too cheap to date when he makes you feel like a two dollar whore instead of a million dollars. I don't care if you are walking up & down a pavement on Hollywood & Vine to support yourself because no-one has ever taken the time to show you your potential, a real good man will make you feel like a million dollars. Yes, reference 'Pretty Woman' if you must. So bounce baby girl I don't care if he is a millionaire this dude is dirt cheap!

7 Cardinal Sins of Dating
Hell No! He Didn't!

"So your sister is hot, what about we all hook up?" He mused.

So I am not a prude by any stretch of your taut imaginations but I will tell you what I am not...a fool! There is naughty, there is kinky and then there is downright disrespectful. If you are 50 years and one foot the grave *gimme me a break!* Check your old ass at the door and learn some order! Discover the 7 Cardinal Sins To Dating. *Hell No* He Didn't!

#1 Thou shalt not hook up with a girl then tell her you are 'just friends'! So he wants to be just friends? Cool beans! He needs to tell you before you spend the weekend in Vegas together! Especially the trusted "old friend" trick! Only a desperate old sod would play that card! Wicked at best! He is hitting the last run as an ok dude before he is an old fart but still running game like the youngling?! We are all sophisticated here, so please spare my girl the lecture after the hook up. If your intentions are as white as snow spit your shit before the fact and watch how long she kicks it with you. But to preach morality, as a wolf in sheep's clothing, warrants mighty contempt!

#2 Thou shalt not hook up with the sister! Blood is thicker than water and so don't be all thirsty trying to hook up with two sisters LOL. Firstly, the only place for a man who would come between a girl and her own flesh and blood, for cheap thrills, with a stupid girl at home, is Dante's Inferno! The 9th circle! The circle of treachery! The last and hottest part of hell! Say Hello to Judas for me will ya!

#3 Thou shalt not chase other women in another woman's presence. Now I understand that you are hard pressed and the only times you get out your are like the monster on S- Street! *"Cookie! Cookie! Cookie!"* But if you invite some-one to spend time with you, please hold your wild horses in their presence. It is rude, disrespectful and above all totally worthy of retaliation. Indeed revenge is a dish best served cold. *"Man head on a silver plate with a glass sweet wine Ma'am?!"* Under the same umbrella is describing the girl you are cheating on to this other woman as perfect! "N" please learn some cheating manners!

 # 4 Thou shalt not try to *run* broken down game! It's one thing to run game it's another to walk it with a broken foot! After all, all *is* fair in love a war. But an old man running a broken down game that plays like an old record and thinking he is badass?! The only one listening might be the deaf young girl he left at home!

#5 Thou shalt not get a big head! So she tells you that the sun and moon shine from your A-hole and that you are the best ever?! Then you take that and run...to her sister! Please! *Lord have mercy.* Truth is you *alright* for what you are! An aging, Latino Casanova who has wronged the wrong bitch. Father, forgive him not for he has sinned!

#6 Thou shalt not ignore texts. Your call boys! Either pay in cash or in kind. By that I mean if you want to be cheap then be prepared to put in real "emo quality time!" But to be cheap then aloof?! If you think anything is for free then you have another thing coming! The least of which is a drama tab to be paid *in full!* Thank-you!

#7 Thou shalt not pull one over her eyes! I mean let's see your game plan. **Break her down. Take what you want. Then Bounce**. Ok, granted its your prerogative to be a fool. But how about you understand that for every action there is a reaction and for 7 of the above mentioned cardinal sins, there is a hell of a price to pay! P.S Yes! Bloggers blog and apparently players play! :)

Hell Hath No Fury
Like A Woman Scorned!
10 Reasons Why He Doesn't Want To
Make You Mad In The Age Of Facebook.

"Dear Wall! Here is a picture of me and Kevin In Paris Last Week!" She Facebooked

So in the beginning was a woman and the woman was with a man and the woman was loved by a man and it was so was so. Then came the kids, the other woman, or the dropping breasts. The woman was without the man and the man was without love for the woman and thus the Garden of Eden and the romantic paradise was no more.

A snake slithering around in the club in a skank dress asked the man to dance. Indeed, it was the man and not the woman whom the devil tempted and eats of the juicy forbidden fruit he did; over and over and over again. God seeing what man had done, taken advantage of the helper whom he had created from him own rib, so that he would be with a mate and not alone was not pleased.

Many years went by and man grew cockier and wicked and thought that he had played even God himself a fool. Then it came to pass that a woman was with child and the child's name was Mark Zuckerberg and thus a modern-day savior was born. Mark was neither very handsome nor blessed with prowess on the basketball court, but he had many gifts of a virtual kind. And thus Facebook was born.

Hell Hath No Fury Like A Woman Scorned! 10 Reasons Why He Doesn't Want To Make You Mad In The Age of Facebook!

#1 Watch him burn when you Twit him snoring laying on your chest as you say *cheese* into the camera, at the world and at his girl at home!

#2 Watch him burn when you make a friend request to his #1 Lady so that she can see all the pictures you have posted of the two of you in your "vacation" folder the same dates as the business trip he took last year.

#3 Watch him burn when You Post What He likes to change into...your dress, on his wall where all his work colleagues can finally agree that *"they knew it!"* before you told. The wonderful thing about a Facebook wall is it's like a real wall. Though he might Deny! Deny! Deny! it. The shit stains will remain and people will always wonder...."*what if?!*" *Mmmmmh!*

#4 Watch him burn when you block him as your Facebook friend but add ALL hs friends. He can ask them what you are posting if he likes!

114

#5 Watch him burn even if he is not on Facebook lol Well guess what? Everyone else he know is so Twit, Twit, Twit!

#6 Watch him burn when his woman's brother gets wind of your posts and decides to call him a little visit Man To Man.

#7 Watch him burn when the fortune 500 company looking to hire him goggles his name and your crying face comes up. No matter how crazy you are bitch the dude can't be right messing with you in the first place?! Right?! Right! :)

#8 Watch him burn when your twits make him so infamous he can no longer run game in over 50 states, 196 countries nor be untruthful in any of 6 500 languages spoken in the world today.

#9 Watch him burn when you see his new profile online in a decade, God willing you both are still alive, kicking and in his case weeping. You'll still have your swagger he will have finally settled for a girl from Africa who doesn't know what Facebook is or be paying for his baby ma to forgive his indiscretions, either way pathetic. You win,

#10 Watch him burn waiting for your virtual retaliation when perhaps one will never come... googling his name daily and checking your tweets and Facebook postings.... For indeed the anticipation of death is worse than death itself.

Your Milkshake Should Bring Boys To The Yard Even After Its Expiration Date!

"I'm sorry Ma'am I think you're past your expiration date!" He exclaimed.

Q1 So who puts the 'expiration date' on women? With milk it's the dairy. I sure as hell know it's not our mamma or even us but men! Yes, the peanut gallery, that is now officially all fired, may no longer tell you when your milk is sour honey. Funny how men can be bad tasting, bad-smelling, and bad-looking but check the expiration date and ...yes you guessed it right. Still good! Here you come along little mamma, spring chicken still in your step, well-preserved, looking good! You know how to cook, take care of a family, handle your man and yet... you've expired?! *"Get the hell out of dodge!"* Honey you had better reset your own date and stop listening to other folks. Trust me when it's your time and you are shitting in your diapers you'll know but until then... *"Your milk shake brings all the boys to the yard and damn right!"*

Q2 How long after the 'sell by' date is an opened container of milk good? So in other words how long after you lose your virginity are you good for? Honey you only get better! Better body as you ripen, better brain as you mature and better technique as you practise!

Q3 How long after the 'sell by' date is an unopened container of milk good? I'd love to lie to you girls and say forever but that is not the case. Men are so twisted sister that if you are still unopened by 40 they will consider you expired and past your sell by date. Funny thing is when you are young they call you a slut if you open up and when you are old they call you an old prune. It's a lose/lose game if you dare to play by their rules...so play by your own!

Q4 So can he drink expired milk? Hell Yeah! He can drink it, he can play with it, splash in it or churn it to cheese! Only bad milk I've ever heard of is milk sitting on the shelf getting bitter. So will the real men please stand up and show these young hustlers what a woman who has matured like a fine bottle of *a Bordeaux, a 1787 Chateau Lafite* tastes like?! And of course I don't expect to see a glass of this exception in the hands of each and every punk. Too rare, too expansive and too a sophisticated acquired taste for your run of the mill player.

Q5 Why does organic *milk* have so much longer (later) 'expiration dates' than regular *milk*? Because like my mamma always told me *it pays to be good.* In the long run living a clean, healthy life, nothing in access (men included) and taking good care of yourself, pays off. If regular girls want to party the boys from their yards then good! The more and the merrier for you!

Q6 Can you drink *milk* on the same day as the "*expiration* date"? So it's your 40th birthday N trying to get with you?! Well if he can do it on that day don't be listening to his "*you've expired!*" lip a few months down the path. If you are good to drink on your so-called expiration date you are good to drink period!

Q7 How do you freeze expired milk? Boob job!, Botox!, facelift, Reslin, Work out, Eat Right, Be in Good standing with the people in your life and God, Make peace with the past and above all forgive. Never stop following your dreams and you'll always have a pulse a real good man can love honey.

Q8 Why does milk expire? Because that's how God made us. Eventually it's time to go. Unless you are a vampire you have a for sure real expiration date...the one that God gave you. On that day we will be crying for your ass. So until then celebrate the gift of life and celebrate you and the changes in you at each and every stage! 30, 40, 50, 60, 70, 80, 90 and God willing 100! If you live to be old and wise and sane...advising your grandchildren, an oral of the past and biding your time to be with your creator then how dare you think you have expired!

You are still the biggest blessing to those who love you?! Men! Shame on you! You are destroyers of women on so many levels it's not even funny. Stop telling women that they are too old; in the words of Lincoln paraphrased, "... *that woman is the best of her kind to the kind of man who loves her kind!"*

Q9 What are the advantages of drinking milk after its 'expiration date'? To quote the Master Ben Franklin: a) because as they have more knowledge of the world and their minds are better stored with observations, their conversation is more improving and more lastingly agreeable, b) because when women cease to be handsome they study to be good. To maintain their influence over men, they supply the diminution of beauty by an augmentation of utility.

They learn to do a thousand services small and great, and are the most tender and useful of all friends when you are sick. Thus they continue amiable. And hence there is hardly such a thing to be found as an old woman who is not a good woman. c) Because there is no hazard of children, which irregularly produced may be attended with much inconvenience.

Q10 What are the side effects if milk is expired? Granted it might be a tad bit bitter at first but if you can realize you now have some good cream on your hands yummy! So ladies chin up and remember even though you might be way past your socially fixed, man dictated, so-called "*expiration date*"...your milkshake will *always* bring the boys to the yard as long as you believe it. Whether those boys be lovers, children or grandchildren or all of the above is entirely up to you.

When Feeling Bad Is Very Good

"Why?!" She cried

My whole life I remember my mother telling me "*Ain't no point crying honey! No-one ever solved a problem nor build a bridge with tears.*" Mother was right in the context of trying to toughen me up before "the real world" took a swing at me but in the literal sense she was wrong. I beg to differ. We live in a society in which we want the ying without the yang. We want to harvest in all seasons, but we cringe at the idea of laboring to grow. We want sunny skies but we dread the rain.

We want instant wealth forget the hard work. We want to live forever botoxed and wearing Christian Louboutin. We want to win yet no-one wants to lose and we want to love without experiencing any pain at all. Well it doesn't work that way. Embrace death, hard work, old age, pain, the dry spells and hard times and you will gain an appreciation for all the good times and find true joy. We live life open to just half of what life is all about then wonder why we are half satisfied.

Discover 10 Times when feeling bad is very good.

#1 Laugh when you cry. Crying is the act through which your soul excretes the liquid by-product of all the pain you silently feel. It is your body's way of allowing you to begin to let go and release the toxins of hurt. You can pretend to be happy forever and lie to yourself but when you find yourself breaking down in heavy sobs it's time to listen to your heart. Make changes for the better. Tears are the first step towards laughter so embrace them.

#2 Be Happy when you feel sad. Sadness is a barometer of emotional change. The lowest key on a musical scale it demands instinctively to be countered by a higher octave of feeling. Sadness is the most accurate indicator that all is not well in *"the state of Denmark"* as it were. Absent of sadness you might remain forever in the shadow of yourself. So when you feel sad in a relationship be very happy because that is you telling yourself to prepare to move on.

#3 Feeling jealous is a great force for revitalization! Although I confess I often preach it, even I am getting tired of this *"New Age"* mumbo jumbo! *Be open-minded. Don't be jealous. Be cool. Be not human!* Jealousy is a healthy emotion! I could write an entire book on just each of these emotions but lightly jealousy is a complex and raw emotion. Artists have explored it in writing, psychologists have exploited factors that result in it, theologians have offered their religious views on it and biologists say that chemical elements in our make-up unconsciously influence it. Concisely, it is a healthy emotion to be reminded of the fact that, that which you value and love dearly and often times take for granted, might be lost to you.

Here is the secret to leveraging jealousy to your advantage... use it as a catalyst to be more considerate, caring and loving. Use it as a cue to revamp the romance in your life and remind your other half that they still mean the world to you.

#4 Envy is motivating. *"Oh, look at her booty! she must be working out! Time to hit the gym!" "Check out that dude... wow! Time to get rid of my dead beat!" "Is that her car?! Where is the line to college again?"*

Nothing like a little envy to get you onto the right track. Envy is just the difference between what some-one else has and what you can get if you set your mind to it. It is in the very genes of our humanity to be motivated by competition to be the alpha. In our sublime minds is the understanding that it is primarily survival of the fittest.

I believe in God, the white man with a beard in the sky, but for the rest of you intellects believe this. Your emotions are the closest to God you will ever get. Especially your negative emotions. They are indeed omnipresent, omnipotent and omniscience. They have the power to transform your life if you pay heed to them.

#5 Anger is delayed pro-action. If you are not proactive in your affairs things happen. He cheats. He lies. He leaves. Anger is a reaction to things happening which are outside of your control. However, you are in your control when you take action. When you prescribe how your life should go there is only those who support your journey and join you or those who *you* leave behind. Anger is the reminder that you need to take action and stop sitting around waiting for him to mess up and then to blame him.

#6 Fear is your spiritual navigation. Of course fear is concern with what we cannot define or quantify. The ever-looming unknown. In times of fear you are forced to be introspective to your core. What is it you hold on to in these times? For everyone the answer will differ. Use fear as a crucial bridge to reconnect with your inner strength. You will need this inner person for battles ahead so don't run away from training, arming and trusting your inner strength.

#7 Disgust is your moral compass. So it makes you sick? It makes your skin crawl? Honey then it's wrong! In a politically correct world sometimes, intellectually it's hard to distinguish between right and wrong. To each his own. If it feels wrong to you don't do it.

Don't take your girls man. Don't cheat on him and don't have a one night stand and wake up feeling dirty. Modern is not another word for ultra dumb. Stand by your morals and they will stand by you down the aisle someday I bet.

#8 Hate is unrequited love. It is true that the opposite of love is indifference. Hate is just the yang to love. Hate catapults you into quick recovery. It helps you skip some emotional stages after a break up. Apathy is the worst place to be because this is the zero before the one on the negative emotional tone scale.

Even I concede that there is nothing good about not caring. The only other state lower than that is death. Not caring and not breathing.

#9 Grief is the healing balm of a wound. If you have loved and lost then you have grieved. This period is frustrating because it takes as long as it takes to recover from your third degree burns to the heart. Allow yourself to grieve and keep a journal. Grief will often unlock latent gifts of poetry, of music or of writing. These are the gifts from the God of your emotions to comfort you and to be a companion to you and to help you self-heal. These in turn can be your gifts to the world if you capture them during this dark period and cultivate them.

#10 Pain is the most effective teacher. If it hurts good enough chances are you won't be stepping into the fire anytime soon. When everything is good it is very hard to grow as a person. Growth is usually in the painful phase and comes with pruning of dead shots just like a gardener tending to his roses before they come into full bloom.

You must compute into your equation of love the down side. You will need to plough the ground. This is a metaphor for breaking through all your fears and limitations and being the best you can be.

You must plant the right seed in the right soil. Your wisdom through experience will be called into effect. You must practice patience which is of course the virtue of Saints and smart bitches. You must cut away everything else. The baggage, the bitterness and the regrets. Cut. Cut. Cut.

You must water with all that is good for you. Self love, continually working on yourself and surrounding yourself with those things which are an asset to you.

Everything else is a liability. Things either add to your value or subtract from it. No force acting on you in life is immaterial so consider the cost and reward. Finally the birthing of something beautiful and new in of itself can be the most excruciating pain you'll ever feel. Here in the valley is the mountain. The character, the loyalty and the very foundation of forever.

So enjoy feeling bad because it's very good for you.

50 Shades of Grey
10 Things Not To Do After You Read It

"I know what I'm doing... I read *50 Shades of Grey*"

If one man can be singularly held responsible for destroying the true delicate world of dominant/subordinate (dom/sub) relationships it is E.L. James the author of *50 Shades of Grey*. For all those behind the pack, this erotic novel chronicles the relationship between a college graduate, Anastasia Steele, and a young business magnate, Christian Grey. It is notable for its explicitly erotic scenes featuring elements of sexual practices involving bondage/discipline, dominance/submission, and sadism/masochism (BDSM).

Enjoy reading the novel, but beware of the underbelly within society this unturned rock might reveal. In order to survive the completion of the saga, here are 10 things not to do after you read *50 Shades of Grey.*

#1 Do Not Let A Stranger Tie You Up For Fun.

For those of you preserving your innocence like my good friend Tina, this is a brand new world filled with things you never imagined in your trashiest wet dreams. There is far more to sexuality than meets the conservative eye. And to those newbies full of wonder and excitement you should of course embrace these new sexually charged thoughts and explore their reality. The problem is dom/sub relationships are not to be either treated lightly or entered into in jest.

Personalities with the proclivity for this play can be far from emotionally stable or "normal" and might take you into the deep end before you have learned how to swim. With that said do not suddenly become comfortable with the thought of being tied up for fun. Tied up is still tied up with everything there in suggested. Just watch the news if you don't understand being restrained against your will can get very scary very quickly. Trust is key. If you don't really trust him don't do it.

#2 Do not respond to creepy DOM ads online – not for one stands.

True there are some legit Doms and Subs out there but unfortunately they are going to have to work even harder to find each other now that all the odd kids have come out to play. A Dom/Sub relationship is a very complex emotional/mental/psychological connection and not to be entered into lightly – not advised as a one night stand. Be very afraid for your life if a guy you just met has rope, duck tape and a copy of *50 Shades of Grey* on his back seat. He is a newbie to this world and you are the experiment that could very well go very wrong.

#3 Dom/Sub relationships are not Bully/Bullied relationships.

Assholes are assholes please don't be fooled into thinking your jerk of a boyfriend was really a secret Dom all along. Being treated like shit and beat up and feeling crappy outside the enigmatic pre consensual bubble of this relationship is still good old fashioned battery. Dial 911.

#4 Do Not think 50 Shades Makes You An Expert.

A Dom/Sub relationship is a actually one of deep emotions and feelings which perhaps best demonstrate the truest state of selfless love. A true Dom is tuned into the complex psychic needs of his sub and only does what the sub allows even though on surface it might not appear to be so. A true Dom is the sub serving the needs of a passive Dom because it takes more strength to submit than to dominate. The dichotomy herein revealed is the essence of what a lot of people will simply not "get" this lifestyle by reading one book. 50 Shades opens the curtain slightly. If you are intrigued begin your education and learn more. You are in kindergarten.

#5 Do Not Go Out and Spend A Fortune on Lifestyle Toys...

Your cash is better spent taking some classes or going to a Dom Convention and getting to learn the scary job of administering pain or hurt on another human being. Manslaughter is still manslaughter and murder is still murder. No matter what the other person insists, define your own boundaries. Safety should be of essence and this comes from knowledge, so get ready to spend time educating yourself. No, it's not as easy as just throwing someone in a cage, slapping them around and action. Professional Dungeon Doms spend years learning how to tie the correct knots amongst other things.

#6 Do Not Discuss With Work and Church Folks

Trust me after this little rush of acceptable openness in the wake of the book passes people will go back to "normal" and you'll just be the weirdo who wants to be peed on. If you need to chat and ask questions join an online community anonymously and then when you grow out of this phase you nickname will not be potty mouth pun intended.

#7 Do Not Share Your Copy Of 50...

Yes your roommate can figure out your sick twisted mind by the dog ears and underlined passages and yes it is very disturbing and should be your private thoughts. No one who loves you will feel comfortable looking at you over dinner later. Yes they read the book to but hell yeah they will be judging you for having purchased the shared copy.

#8 Don't Get Drunk To Experiment

If you do not appreciate that both parties are making themselves extremely vulnerable by entering this arrangement don't do it. A Dom is holding a life in his hands and a Sub is letting someone hold their life in their hands. This should be a sober decision.

#9 Don't Go From Zero to Piercings...

Or any other permanent body alterations you might regret after the fad has died.

#10 Don't denounce the relationship you are in as boring

You just might need a shoulder to cry on when it's all said and done and you come running home.

Hand Job That Gets the Ring and 10 That Don't

Will You Marry Me?" He Whispered

"I do!" She responded with a soft cry.

So you want to basically give me the finger right? After all who am I to tell you why you don't have a wedding ring! Listen I apologize because I have been MIA. I missed you too. I just didn't feel like I was being true to my readers chained to my desktop all day. The most important part about being a relationship blogger is throwing caution to the wind and actually having relationships! Lol Yes, men or women if that's your cup of tea. Just hard to do when I know better. But I would never dare to sit in an ivory tower and preach.

So here we are again together during the loneliest time of the year... the holidays! Nothing Ho ho ho here, but those poor girls still standing at the street corners. I have travelled to the peaks of the mountains and come back wiser. Yes men are still nothing but a hound dog. No matter which way you slice it, the result is the same. Be well aware of love. Beware.

So back to my hand job... no pun intended. I am going to work with you through this block on the most important thing to consider when waiting for a wedding ring... what kind of hands are you sitting around on waiting.?! Here are 10 types of hands and only one gets the ring.

#1 The whore hand does not get the ring. Those nasty ass "I am too poor to afford acrylic nails and so when I get them done I try not to cut them off" hand does not get the ring! Seriously? Try changing diapers with those things! Try cleaning the house or just touching your man... right... and forget about cleaning yourself up properly without bleeding to death. A smart man will run! You're a nasty girl and those are some one night stand nails! Next!

#2 Then there is the cheap hand. The one we've all had with flaking nail polish and half broken nails. Girl please! How can you even imagine a diamond ring on that? Next!

#3 The man hand, I'm sorry, is a curse. You can only keep it out of sight! Don't take pictures with it showing your age leaning into it because you copied the poise from some-ones else with lean, feminine hands. Don't pat him squarely on his hand during dinner to sympathize. Keep that Man hand out of sight and rub him on his back or if you are close thighs instead. Show him that you are capable and that is sexy but forget the pageant wave honey because you are waving your own engagement ring bye-bye!

132

#4 The ghetto hands with too much decorations and stones and faces going on will get you nothing but a ghetto ass man! What is wrong with you? Showing him you can't pick nail polish or you are possessed by a legion is not going to cut it. Be Vogue. One solid flattering nail polish. Something that compliments your skin complexion and gives it a glow and viola!

#5 The "I'm all bones and don't know where my next meal is coming from" hand is not cute! No one wants to imagine you little Miss Anorexia dying due to breast feeding! Gimme a break! Eat!

#6 But chunky girls before you break out into a full blown smile hold your horses Missy! The "Oh I'm a little piggy with no self control when it comes to excessive eating" hand is not cute either! Be within your height/weight appropriate range and work it out! So he can with the jewelry store!

#7 For all the dark skinned girls using lighteners and forgetting your crazy looking darker hands, stop it!

It screams 'I'm insecure,' it's ugly, and it's darn right weird. No man wants to marry a zebra complexion; decide what race you are! I suggest that unless you want to end up like Michael Jackson, you pick your God-given race.

#8 The jittery shaking hand indicative of a drug addict won't cut it either. No one wants this person for a wife; kick your habits. It's 2019!

#9 The nail bitten bloody spades of a nervous hand will never get a ring. It screams of all your insecurities and childhood and apparently adulthood trauma, so stop it! Let him discover your full ill graces with time as you fight the good fight of being a better person!

#10 So now that you know the hand job that does not get the ring what gets the big sparkling sapphire, ruby, or diamond? Well, it's the opposite of that fancy rock. It's the simple hand. Keep your nails short neat and if they must be long just a few inches of you no plastics for 2019.

A well taken care of hand bespeaks of a woman of great character, attention to detail and grace. Having your nails and toes "on point" shows the basic maintenance of self dictated by holding down some job and being consciousness of decorum.

Mmmmmh, starting to sound like "wifey" material? This is the hand you can take home to mom. This is a hand not afraid to get dirty or do some hard work. This is the helping hand of a life time long companion. Keep your nails polished and steer away from bright red "hooker" nail polish pick more subtle soft colors, but when you are truly ready keep your nails bare.

This shows an untouched fresh innocence which every man looks for in his wife – the soft gentle hand that will rock a baby's cradle. The strong supportive hand that will sooth and encourage your man through the storm of life.

The capable hardworking miracle kissed hand that will manifest cough syrup to heal the sick and food to feed the multitudes; the hand that will feed the poor and make a difference in the world; the hand that will leave the mark of a great woman.

Ladies this is the hand which gets: "I do!"

Put Your War Paint On!
Because Baby Love Is War!

"Indeed, all is fair in love and war" she said without expression.

The difference between my married girlfriends and my single ones is simple...the married ones are great military general, strategist and tactician. Love is a war and not for the faint of heart. You will suffer many tragic loses and near devastation. You will be humiliated to the point of retreat and your waterloo will be a broken heart but in the words of one of the greatest generals Theodore Roosevelt: "Far better it is to dare mighty things, to win glorious triumphs even though chequered by failure, than to rank with those poor spirits who neither enjoy nor suffer much because they live in the gray twilight that knows neither victory nor defeat".

So, here are 10 reasons to put on your war paint this holiday ladies because we are going to win the battle and win the war!

135

#1 Strategic Planning and Rational Analysis: All of you are single because you have not planned to be otherwise. You have wished, hoped, prayed and dreamt it. That would not have won the war for Alexander the great. Sit down with your closest confidant and advisory council and like in my Shona Culture plot out the demise of his bachelorhood. The how will be discussed later so just scroll through and get the guidelines on romance.sex, men and relationships.

#2 Importance of Information and Related Processing Capability: So the same way a General with undisciplined soldiers won't win the war the same applies to you. If I were you I would look to this book and other self help books for pearls of wisdom. Consider the source...an ex, a jealous girlfriend or an ignorant misinformed co-worker will not win you the war.

#3 Importance of Knowledge, Wisdom and Understanding: of a man and what makes him tick. Stop projecting unless he was a woman in a past life you will learn nothing about him from other women. Ask your trusted guy friends; "Seven Dwarfs" as per my blog, and they will be your best source. Also read Steve Harvey's book, *Think Like A Man, Act Like A Lady*".

#4 Study The Past, Market Analysis, Develop And Maintain An "Edge": With the plethora of debilitated relationships you certainly have enough examples of what not to do!

#5 Staying Focused On Strategic Objectives: "To Get Your Man!" Don't give up on me! Let's take all the fabulous drama that's you into 2019 and I promise you that I will help you find the man of your dreams!

136

#6 Suitability of Strategies and Tactics to Situation: Match the suitability of strategies and tactics to the market's phase, section, pattern, and volatility. For instance the market phase for a good man is that we have hit a global recession so you will need to up your game!

#7 Inherent Advantages and Disadvantages: Understand, and guard against, the inherent disadvantage in every advantageous situation. Likewise, be alert to capitalizing on advantages that occur in distressed situations. So if he just broke up with his ex your approach will be completely different to some-one who is single and has being for a long time. A divorcee is not a widower.

#8 Opportunistic Flexibility in Adapting Strategies and Tactics to Situation: Be ever diligent to switching it up because no two days are the same in love and in war.

#9 Ethical Conduct: Be moral and ethical in all things: so no married men with kids, or stealing other people's men or cheating with your BFF's man. This is a short term battle victory, but this will never win you the war!

#10 Rely On Your Own Preparation: Be on point cross your T's and...! Because if you think that he has escaped commitment by chance for this long and you will just waltz in from the streets and become his woman you are in for a rude awakening! He is a master strategist who has guarded his heart fiercely for 2, 3, 4 or 5 decades! Girl, get your weapons of mass destruction out because it is going to be World War 4 to win his heart.

#11 Competent Management: Where the matters of your heart are concerned and managing them you are going to have to put on your thinking hat. Hire the best parts of your logic this is not a game it is life or death. It is the war known as love. And to the conqueror goes the spoils and they shall be spoilt by their rich new fab hubby! Once they win him over of course.

#12 Disciplined Emotions: Feel little to nothing even though you are in love with him as this will weaken you. Love him enough to feel nothing and allow him to feel everything!

#13 Disciplined Organization and Financial Management: Discipline, efficient, and effective organization, and utilization of all resources (people, plans, tools, capital), in the capacity to which they are best suited, in all situations, is critical to success. It will take an army!

#14 Clear Communication: Let him know you want him, then retreat. He has been forewarned right? :) Right!

#15 Deception and "Shaping": Not the immoral kind but they how many men have you been with kind of lie.... a gentleman would never ask a lady would never answer. You are well within your defensive rights to divide the number by 2 and then subtract plenty away!

#16 Avoidance of Being Deceived and "Shaped": If you are sick and tired of being deceived get with the program. Stop listening to his lies and start telling your own!

#17 Reward, Replenish and Invest in a Support Structure: If it works for you, keep it up! Whether it's your non-possessive nature, your humor or your looks, reinvest in these areas of fortification even long after the war is won.

#18 Patience, Positioning and Timing: Rome was not build in a day even though in the past you allowed yourself to be conquered in a day. If you want forever slow your roll.

#19 Avoidance of Catastrophic Loss: Never be caught cheating, stealing and outright lying.

#20 Preservation and Protection of Resources: If you don't trust her off with her head. If he betrays you off with is head. Keep it moving and never settle. Be ruthless in this policy because only then can you ever plan to conquer true love.

Love is an Equation
10 Rules to Help You to Do the Math and Find the Perfect Man

"In love you take a chance." She pondered.

Love is a matter of the heart which must be calculated with the head. In a relationship, there are things which add value, mistakes that subtract trust, situations which divide intimacy, so basically love is an equation.

Here are 10 Rules to Help You Do The Math.

#1 Add value to your relationship by treating it as a third person. It's no longer you and him it's the "us" "Us" is a brand new person on the planet and greatly resembles an infant. Like an infant tender, gentle nurturing care is essential to grow an affair to maturity. Just like in raising a child the input of both partners will determine what your love grows into. Is it confident and trusting or is it delinquent and insecure? Carefully add only those things which you would give to your own offspring to rear success.

#2 Subtract trust by lying and breaking trust. Any hurtful actions to the contrary of whatever your unique personal agreements that take away the value of love. Unfortunately sometimes the rate of depreciation is more rapid than the appreciation and that's when you have no choice but to call it a sad day.

#3 Multiply every ingredient that your partner expresses love for. Bring home more roses, keep things neater around the house, wear sexy lingerie more often or bring more Bedroom Kandi to the bedroom. In the back of your mind, see these things as a savings account for a rainy day. It just might keep you together and save your love.

#4 Divide the potential for a long future together by being disagreeable, fighting or cheating. Be careful of even seemingly whimsical fleeting indiscrete thoughts. Unconquered temptation will gain a mental stronghold on you which will turn to obsession and ignite into behavior. So tame your mind to let your enviable love run spectacular and wild.

#5 Simplify things to the lowest common denominator for the best kiss. Listen, nothing in life is that complicated. We are born. We live. We die. Take any problem and you can attribute it to the business of living or/and the business of dying. The hyphen in life before death is love. So be smart and do the math!

"I hate you!" Said her lover he meant "I love you and that is why I'm so hurt" A simple genuine sorry is *the* solution.

Let's do another love equation..

"I don't care! Do whatever you want! Said his lover she meant "I feel like I care too much and it's all one sided... Give me a reason to believe in you again through your actions. Do the love thing... Hug me. Kiss me hold me"

You figure out this love equation by yourself.

"I don't believe in love anymore! It's just a fairytale." Her lover said.

The answer is simple.

#6 Take to the power 2 the basic truths you fundamentally have in common this will give them an infinite power. In love you will need a strong common foundation to build a lasting relationship.

#7 Round off any mistakes to the nearest wholesome memory you have of each other. Forgive twice as much you would like to be forgiven ad infinite. This is the secret to forever.

#8 Do not leave problems unsolved as this will only create irreconcilable differences. If it's a long division problem use this rule of thumb simplifies both sides of both peoples dilemma and suddenly the solution will appear.

#9 As life happens and things get added, subtracted, multiplied and so forth it can get confusing. The best solution to this mixed equation is to create solvable like terms. Find new hobbies, travel or spice things up in the bedroom with Bedroom Kandi... Anything totals to a lot in keeping a surplus in the relationships feel good account.

#10 The ancient equation in love is a sacred math through which we solve the biggest problem of our existence... Why are we here? Why does it hurt? Why does it feel so good?

Why do we laugh? Cry? Fail? And triumph? ... as the delicate notes in the majestic symphony of our lives. And the answer is simple. Because we can! 'The ability to' is our gift through life of creations love. So do the math in your life today and if you are not happy balance this simply equation and make it right.

The DNA of Love
10 Astounding Things You Should Know!

"Honey, I'm sorry I love you but not the way you want me to." He said to his younger lover.

At first glance it might seem impossible that an intelligent, good-looking older man might not be madly in love with his much younger exotic goddess of a girlfriend. She is brilliant, inspired, adores him and they have the kind of energy which makes impossible dreams come true. Once or twice in a lifetime if you are blessed you might make this kind of a love connection... unfortunately it often happens later in life as it takes wisdom to distinguish pebbles from pearls.

But if we had a magical microscope and could find the smallest indivisible particle of an atom of love we just might discover its mysterious DNA coding. Here are 10 astounding things which will take your breath away about the DNA of love.

#1 The state of love is an evolutionary process which began long before bloggers like me and the glossy covers of Vogue had a quick 10 tips to make him love you. At some point in early ages it become an advantage for pair bonding to ensure the survival of the young as the 9 months of pregnancy and subsequent child birth and rearing would take a lot out the human female. So it is hard wired into our DNA coding pro survival for us to have aspirations towards monogamous pairing. Please note my realistic not cynical use of the verb "trying".

As gender roles evolve and change it is no longer strictly necessary for two people to raise a child. (Even though as a single mom I can attest that it has taken an entire village in my case I was blessed to have the solid support of family.) Given the changes in our world today I would not be surprised if monogamy becomes a mythical human quality in the distant DNA coding future.

#2 The reasons why women feel a need for love is also to be found in our DNA hard-coding with all roads leading to procreation of the human race. Men who seem to have much more difficulty in committing to situations can finally blame is on science. Indeed, their prototypes role was to simply spread the seed and keep in next to moving.

#3 Understanding why you love his old, balding head and fat ass while he requires you to work out and look good will be easily explained by referring to the DNA of love once again. Women love security and men love women and so the world goes round. Don't feel bad.

Gold digger is a modern word in prehistoric terms I might hail you as the amazing, wise, all-knowing womb from which the Homo sapiens evolved. It is believed that our race comes from those proceeding ancestors that were wise enough and lucky enough to end up in a climatically favorable part of the earth. AKA "The best neighborhood that was around!" I dare say a woman had something to do with that.

"Honey, I just refuse to live in these average size caves and next to "those people!" We have younglings running around and more on the way and I want them to go hunting where there is good game and swim in clean rivers. Babe, are you listening to me! Please stop watching that barbaric spot where you all pile up kicking dead lions heads! I just don't get you sometimes!"

#4 Another group classification in the DNA of love is which stage you are in life. The first innocent love of children does not have the same biological demands of young adult love nor the less physical companionship factors shared by people later in life. In the best phase of course which the ripe wise age you delightfully realize that there is more to heaven and earth than meets the eyes. Until then you spend half your life trying to meet someone and the other half hoping to get rid of them.

"Honey, I'm sorry I love you but not the way you want me to." He said to his younger lover. Young women with older lovers you cannot generally expect the fever of youth.

For most men and women they are past the reproduction stages and guess what? Surprise! It is harder for them to fall in-love because in our DNA coding it is a waste of evolutionary cells to have SOPs (super old people) copulating. So back to our example he loves you but he does not desire to rip your clothes off and make babies. Either accept it or move on to an age appropriate group.

#5 Another way in which nature teases us and has a great sense of humor is now men desire men and women. I personally I am a very firm Gay advocate and do not think that there is ever justification for any man, woman or child to be treated which anything less than their God given unalienable rights. In terms of our DNA hard coding however this might be in response to the overpopulation crises on the planet as nature would see all these couplings as childless.

#6 Love is therefore nothing more than a voodoo or make believe word we made up to explain things we can now understand. Virtually it in of itself does not exist. Love only exists in the context to which is it sublimely influenced by a trillion variables evolved over time in our hard DNA coding to manifest itself.

#7 Media, literature, repeated self lies and drugs can of course alter how we interpret what happens to us on a chemical level. Somewhere in our enthusiastic pursuits of civilization and socialization, we learnt to disassociate from the very simply basic truth we are at cellular level animals and our life is a chemically engineered response and how we communicate with our internal and external worlds through the semi permeable membrane of our cells.

#8 So ladies, sorry to break it to you. You and your host or coven of girlfriends do not get to pick in love our DNA does all the work.

#9 So now that the pressure to pick is completely out

of your hands, perhaps you can finally surrender and enjoy the journey. We are a product of our environment. If what was pro survival was suddenly little green alien men with big heads and small (smh) you would suddenly hear this conversation...

"I mean he comes from a very good family on Mars. He has the fastest aircraft and I dunno, I think our babies will have my head!"

#10 Ahhh, now that my bashing of humanity is done for the morning, I am going to look forward to seeing my significant other. Who knows why I feel sweaty palms, butterflies and heart back flips. Probably a pre-DNA program to when men brought home the bacon.

But I ate already so overriding my silly giddy senses! Have a gorgeous Love DNA evolutionary day.

Meet Bigger Better Breman!
10 Reasons Why You Should LOL When
He Checks Out Other Women Around You

Now I know we have a met a lot of assholes, but the one who gets the award tonight in honor of the Grammys and our 2nd Anniversary is Bigger Better Bergman! We have all meet this creep who crushes our egos after spending hours of dollars getting ready to go out with him. Well, you will lol when this douche checks out other women whilst out with you and here are 10 reasons why.

#1 I will take him straight to something worse than an early grave, a late life old people's home. Yip, this is where people who can't make up their minds end up: alone sitting in a rocking chair staring at the walls watching paint dry and waiting...praying for death.

#2 Lol because his A.D.D is a curse which will follow him in life. He will still be looking with the next one so don't be hurt she is enjoying it as much as you are.

#3 It is terrible dating etiquette; scratch your ass and wipe your snotty nose on your shirt sleeve whilst you are at Bergs...same thing. I would sit back order the most expansive thing on the menu, top shelf liquor and smile. Bigger Better Bergman thanks for dinner!

#4 Tit for... start making goo-goo eyes at the ugliest guys in the room. Yes Bergs that fat troll is so much more attractive than you.

#5 How can I leave out the classical 'Excuse yourself softly from the table and never return?' Do not pick up his calls or explain why. If you run into him look through him after all you were invisible to his manners now he is invisible to you. Invisible, Bigger, Better, Bergman.

#6 On the karma tip, he will catch a bitch on the back lash. If you keep playing Russian roulette with love...

#7 Bigger Better Bergman is really smaller worse Bergman compared to your ex so next!

#8 BBB is like a headless voodoo chicken escaping a sacrifice! Lol All that head jerking and cockeyed movement..."are you having an anaphylactic attack" or (giggle) "forgive me for laughing I've never dated a squint eyed guy before. It looks like you are looking over there and I'm sitting over here. Weird... anyhow..."

#9 If you are looking for and believe in "Charming" then you have to give hats off to Bigger Better Bergman. Frogs! (smh)

#10 We attract what we are... Bigger Better Bergman doesn't want anyone and the truly sad thing is no one truly wants him either.

I Spy With My Little Eyes
Something Beginning With L
10 Clues He Is Lying To You

"I spy with my little eyes something beginning with L!" She said.

I spy with my little eye something beginning with R! While we may not all have a degree in Criminology or Law, we are all blessed with instinct. If you suspect your man is chasing after someone else's cheese, here are 10 things every LPI (Lady Private Investigator) should know on how to catch that rat!

#1 The Trash Can Never Lies! So you have cursed the house, waited for him to go to work, called his office and confirmed he is in meetings all day. You have switched out your natural locks for a blonde white girl wig, blue contacts and a house keepers outfit. You are ready to scale the wall, disarm the alarm and enter his crib. Your pink Tom Tom's make your Indian name floating feather. Without further ado, dive deep into his trash can.

"Mmmmmmmh something is a-foot!" Yes tampon wraps, make up removers, and yuckie used condoms might indeed be a red flag if you, like cat-woman, have made it this far. Unfortunately, us mere mortals will have to stick to casing the man. To get to know a man, dig up the trash can of his mouth in anger. Most women make the mistake of screaming to be making their point when they should be listening to his! What names does he call you?

What did his ex do that you do? Why is he never home on time, and what is the problem with your weight again? And there you have it. You are being compared to someone he still loves, is in love with or will love in the future. Pack it up. It is only a matter of time now, and a lady never overstays her welcome.

#2 A Closet Never Lies! Now the closet search is not for the faint hearted! If she lives there, or frequents him often, you will find her red bottoms and Hugo Boss here! Oh yeah bitches like this always have the shit you pray for and wish he would get or you....well he can't he is getting it for her! Time for some tough love. Check the drawers as well. No, those are not his clothes that shrank in the washing machine. He has kids! And the hardest thing to find in the closet is your man! Sorry, boo.

#3 A Medicine Cabinet Never Lies! So how long has your man been on birth control? Wow!

#4 A Car Dashboard Never Lies! If that is his favorite juicy couture scent or lipstick color, girl you are in trouble! He has bigger secrets to share with you. You thought he was cheating on you with some girl, but he is the other woman! Run! Next!

#5 A Cell Phone Never Lies! A man's phone is dangerous. You cannot come back from what you will find here. This is no man's land, because what you find here you cannot un-see. Text messages and missed and made call logs are all damning evidence. I once knew an especially bright guy...he tried to convince me that I had read the message wrong. But a smart girl sends all texts to herself to brood over with the pack later. Some flowers and a lot more clever lies later, the truth is that the trust is already lost. This is a two way street. You violated his privacy. He violated your heart. A match made in hell?

#6 A Wallet Never Lies! From credit cards you didn't know he had, to business cards from other women, to all the damning dinner for two receipts when he was having Boys Night Out. Gosh He Must LOVE that boy! That sensation you are feeling is called falling out of love. It is that heart sinking, bile rising in your throat, heart beat slowing down for dead, deep in your belly it is over feeling. The last four steps are just to nail his coffin shut...no-one likes an ex coming back from the dead! They stink!

#7 A Pocket Never Lies! Much like a wallet, a man's pockets always tell on him! Match sticks from some hotel resort, a number scribbled on a paper in pretty writing, and for the real dada heads keys to Motel 6!

#8 A Facebook Status Never Lies! So he wants it to say single. Why? His boss should not care dime! Or those comments from Lucy and Becky no woman is just liking a man for kicks, honey doll. And that "Friend" clinging to him like a drowning man at every major event is not his favorite sister Becky! And the real pigs that block their timelines, so no-one can leave messages, please go and sit down! The other woman's time line is loaded with your photo's and screen shots of all your texts. SMH. Where can a good cheater run and hide these days?

#9 Match.com Never Lies! Baby Doll, his mama did not have two of his ugly ass! That is not his evil uglier twin! Yes it's his big Gucci denying head on Match! His profile reads like... the BS he told you on your first date! He suddenly has a higher income bracket and his unemployable ass is CEO of what? Lies Inc? Ok. So those are lovely pictures taken a few years ago when he was on roids and had a little hair. And that is not a bad look in his friend's boat taken on the lake.

Mmmmmh that suit you got him for his birthday is his best look. He is still 49? And he wants a woman with a college degree and is intelligent, but won't, however, have the mind to catch him at his lies! He last spoke to his mom last Thanksgiving but he is a family man and in his dreams, he loves to race cars for fun. For kicks, create a profile too and respond to him re-introducing yourself and see if the asshole will fall for you twice!

#10 The Heart Never Lies! By the time that you went searching for my book, you already knew. There is no lens that can see deeper than the heart. Yes, you are over 30. Yes, you thought, perhaps. Of course dating is a chore. And it is going to hurt like a rat's ass. What can I say? At least you have the skills to open a very successful Private Investigation firm!

Freebies
Sign up and grab a free audio version of *What Your Mom Didn't Tell You* on Audible.com

Get 20% discount on Chiedza's next book by signing up on her author website: www.blackmoneybrands.com or writing to blackmoneybrands@gmail.com

Also get a free audio version of *What Your Mom Didn't Tell You* by signing up on Audio.com.

For all speaking engagements, please contact Chiedza at blackmoneybrands@gmail.com